GAMBLERS
FOOLS
AND FATE
ON THE
ROAD TO KEY WEST

Michael Reisig

GAMBLERS FOOLS AND FATE
ON THE ROAD TO KEY WEST

ISBN Paperback: 978-1-7363479-3-5
ISBN eBook: 978-1-7363479-2-8

Printed in the United States of America
First Printing, 2021

Dedication

Once again, as always, this book is dedicated to my lady, Bonnie Lee. Without her steadying force, without her insight and dedication to making my life…good…most of this would never have happened. I am far more than grateful for that crossing of stars so many years ago, which I realize clearly now was no accident.

Also, this book is dedicated to a handful of wonderful writers of adventure and Caribbean tales, many of whom I'm proud to say are friends of mine. The support, insight, and friendship we offer each other are gifts beyond price. Wayne Stinnett, John Cunningham, Nick Sullivan, Don Rich, Mike Pettit, Steven Becker, David Wilson, Steve Kittner, Julie Rogers, Virginia Williams, Nicholas Harvey, and Bob Simpson. Sometimes you're the wind…sometimes you're the sails…

I would, of course, be seriously out of line if I failed to mention my editors and good friends, Tim Slaughter (who cleans and sifts the initial tedious hodgepodge of words I give him), and Cris Wanzer (whose final literary magic and incredible insight shapes and molds what I give her into something of which we can all be proud). And I am immensely pleased with my cover designer, Sandra Glassbrook, who gets it right so quickly.

Thank you all for making my life so good!

Introduction

To my readers...

Without giving too much away here, I would like to preface this read with a few words. Most of you who are familiar with my novels know that I generally walk a fine line between accurate but unique environmental and historical details, and controversial concepts yet verified beyond questionable doubt. It's a challenge for me, and on occasion, I sacrifice readers for the pleasure of providing "what-if" situations (and hopefully, stretching minds).

This novel is no different. It expands parameters, asks questions, and represents challenges to what we know and what we don't know for sure about our planet and our universe. But it'll still make you snort with laughter every once in a while and rip at the pages in places.

In addition, the island at the beginning of this book — Coiba, off the coast of Panama — is not imagination or writer's flair. It is absolutely real. Not only is the island itself authentic, with its remarkable, nearly unbelievable flora and fauna, but its history as one of the most bizarre and frightening penal institutions in Central America is also true.

It is a reminder to us all that sometimes real life can be stranger than fiction. And more than anything, I would use this to remind you all that, if not for imagination, if not for our willingness to recognize "the possibilities" in life, on our planet, and in this universe, we might still be living in caves. So don't be afraid to exercise your imagination on occasion, and let your mind grow. *You've got nothing to lose...*

Come take a wild ride with the Hole in the Coral Wall Gang (from the Florida Keys to the Caribbean, and into Central America) and discover the incredible secret of Coiba Island…

— *Michael Reisig*

Terraformation

The term *terraformation* is defined as the hypothetical process of deliberately modifying the atmosphere, temperature, surface topography, or ecology of a planet so that it is similar to the environment of Earth, to make it more habitable by Earth-like life…

CHAPTER ONE

Panama
February 1991

He was sitting alone at a small table at the back of The Blind McCaw Bar in the western coastal city of Playa La Coquita. The Blind Macaw was a humble establishment at best — poorly lit, a little too warm, and a little low rent. Big-bladed fans struggled to cut the gray smoke that clung to the ceiling, and the radio in the back scratched out Spanish melodies of past and present while a melancholy waitress moved between the three occupied tables with the enthusiasm of a sloth. There were five people slouched at the old mahogany bar — a couple of devoted clients and some sun-burnished surfers taking a break from the notorious waves in the area. *Rush hour...* The rest of the clientele looked like something out of a Sam Peckinpah movie. In the whole scene, there was only one fellow that stood out, yet something said to me that he was trying not to.

He was tan, about five foot eight, had shoulder-length dark hair, and was well built but not overly muscular. He was sitting at a table in the far corner, where he could see who came in. There was some Hispanic in his blood (we were in Panama and this sure as hell wasn't a standard tourist stop), but the green eyes said he had some European history as well. The fellow was dressed in blue jeans, a T-shirt, leather sandals, and a nylon windbreaker. By the looks of him, I would have said he wasn't a coward or a hero, but the wariness in his eyes and his attention to everything around him said he'd been around the block a time or two.

It was an almost cool, midwinter evening about eleven o'clock. Things in "La Coca" were winding down, although the only real tourist trade was the American surfers who came for cheap living and good waves. But there was something about the fellow in the corner that said he wasn't here for the waves…or the liquor…or the company. It looked as if he might be appreciating the comfort of anonymity. Having been there and done that on occasion, I recognized the caution in his eyes.

■ ■ ■

Diego Tarras had a history that a fiction writer would have gladly paid for. But he didn't want to share it right now. The young man had paid some prices — serious prices — for the tales he possessed.

He came by his ruddy complexion and green eyes honestly, and spoke English well but with a healthy Spanish accent. His father had been an American from South Florida — the son of one of Teddy Roosevelt's acclaimed Rough Riders, years and years ago. His dad had developed an inclination for southern climes and became a sailor out of Key West — and a part-time smuggler. (Whatever paid best at the time.) He eventually drifted out of the States and down through Central America, ending up in Panama, where he met an attractive courtesan in the coastal city of Colón. She was dark-haired, black-eyed, and beautiful. He was tall and muscled, with a charming disposition for a pirate, and a disarming smile. They found each other and after a month of romance, they came to a compromise. She quit her evening job and he quit the sea, and soon after, they made a son, Diego.

Young Diego was raised on tales of adventure. With a Rough Rider for a grandfather and an occasional brigand as a father, Diego Tarras naturally gravitated to the more adventurous side of life. It wasn't that he was a bad guy, really… It was just that he needed a little "jazz" now and then.

Still, he managed to stay out of the more spurious occupations, finding work as a sailor, as his father had. But one night in Panama City, bad luck and a simple bar fight changed his life forever. Diego was only twenty-one years old when he got into an altercation with a man over a woman. In the process, he hit the guy, hard, and the fellow didn't get up. In fact, he never got up again.

It was an unfortunate situation — self-defense, really. A thirty-second bar fight. In normal circumstances in Panama, Diego might have done a few months in jail, just because. But the guy he killed was the son of one of the district's municipal judges. Not only was Señor Mateo Preces politically powerful, but he had ties to the Panama City underworld. And Mateo Preces was a brutally vengeful soul.

Diego Tarras was given two years in prison. Not just one of the run-of-the-mill mainland prisons, but in the horrible stone fortress called Coiba Island Penitentiary off the western coast of Panama. Originally built in 1919 and controlled at one time by the monster dictator Manuel Noriega, who used it as his personal punishment for political dissenters, it was literally hell on earth.

Those two years were torturous beyond belief. No one expected him to survive, least of all the man who sent him there, but somehow Diego did. The first year, he was sentenced to the stone fortress/prison with the masochistic guards and the isolation of coral rock cells, his only companions being rats and scorpions. During the latter part of the second year, he was released into the island, which might have seemed like a good thing. But you see, there was really no getting away from Coiba, and surviving on the island was a horror story in itself.

But his time on the island, as horrible as it was, came with a strange discovery — a unique, bizarre encounter with luck and timing. It was beyond Diego's imagination or experience, and it challenged the laws of nature and the truths he had always known. But it didn't matter. He had seen what he had seen, and he knew what he knew, regardless of how it twisted his reality.

The problem right now, given the two men staring at him from the distant table, was staying alive until he could figure out a way to sneak back into the hellish island from which he'd just been released. Yes, to sneak back into hell so that he might bring out what would validate his bizarre tale. Talk about bitter kismet…

Unfortunately, upon Tarras' release from Coiba Island Prison, things had gotten worse instead of better. Diego was visiting his parents when he found out the man whose son he had killed had decided that two years in prison was an insufficient price for his child's life. He wanted more — "an eye for an eye" — and he put a price on the young man's head.

When Diego discovered there was money on him, he realized that his only choice was to get out of town. Hell, to get out of Panama, if he wanted a chance to grow old. But he also knew that, at some point, he had to go back to that island. His past and his future converged there in the most astonishing fashion, offering more danger than the common man would remotely consider while dangling a most incredible story and the possibility of unfathomable wealth.

So, for the moment, he was lying low, thinking maybe tomorrow he'd slip across the border into Costa Rica and find a boat that would take him back to Coiba. Back into hell…

■ ■ ■

My partner in misadventure, Will Bell, and I had become bored with the hustle and bustle of Key West during "the season" and in a spur-of-the-moment thing had decided to pack up my Cessna 182 and shoot down to Panama — maybe do a little surfing at the breaks around Santa Catalina on the southwestern coast. We weren't great surfers but we truly loved the sport.

Surfing is like sex — you don't understand it until you've

experienced it. Then you can't wait to do it again. Sliding down the face of a wave, the inertia of Mother Nature hurling you along…the sun in your eyes, your body tense but your senses so completely alive…balance and eyesight at their keenest as you watch the wave morph in front of you and try to stay in sync with it. You know that one mistake, one miscalculation, and you're tumbling out of control underwater, struggling for the surface and that first glorious breath. Surfing. It's just you and Mother Nature in a dance and the music is never the same. I can say these words, but only those of you who have experienced the lure of the waves understand…and you're nodding now and smiling.

Will and I were near the end of a fairly uneventful evening foray in the search for local talent when we drifted into The Blind Macaw. We were having a final nightcap before heading back to our hotel. I continued to study the younger fellow near the back of the bar with the long dark hair and startling green eyes while he watched everyone that came through the door. He was a little too intent about it all, his eyes carrying just a touch of uneasiness.

The guy brought up his drink and Will nodded slightly at him. "What do you think about that one, Kansas?"

"Yeah," I muttered. "The boy's got issues — not happy with where he is exactly, maybe not happy with who he is right now."

"Keeps touching that windbreaker…" Will observed.

I had also noticed that his right hand occasionally brushed the breast pocket of his jacket. It was a "tell" that he could have done without — it spoke of a weapon or something valuable.

After weighing the scene, I noticed there might be more here than met the eye. There were two other guys in the far corner of the bar — also Central Americans. Serious fellows, hard faces, drinking straight tequilas. They were eyeing the guy as well, trying not to appear obvious.

Will took a glance at them and his eyes casually slid back to me. We'd been around the block too many times not to notice the interest.

"Yeah, I know," I said. "But it's not our business."

As if on cue, a small group of surfers came stumbling into the bar, loud, happy, and fairly drunk, carrying the cool evening breeze with them. It was just the diversion the young man with the dark hair and cautious eyes was looking for. As the youngsters moved between him and the seated strangers, he rose and quickly made his way toward the door. In a second, he was gone.

The two fellows in the corner immediately lost all sense of pretense. They were up and headed toward the door.

"That isn't good," I said under my breath, running a hand through my sun-bleached hair nervously.

"Christ!" growled Will angrily as he pushed back his seat. "All I wanted was a couple of drinks and maybe a little horizontal mambo with a cute surfer chick if I was really lucky… Not this cowboy bullshit again." He pushed out a bitter sigh. "I'm getting too old for this crap."

I shrugged. "It's not our business," I repeated. But I couldn't help turning toward the entrance.

The two Latinos were just disappearing. One was reaching into his pocket and I thought I saw the glint of a blade.

Will exhaled hard and rose, pulling that lanky frame of his out of the seat with purpose. "C'mon, Tonto," he huffed. "I'd like to ignore this but I just can't."

"Me, the Lone Ranger," I said, holding up a finger. "You, Tonto."

We got out onto the street just in time to see the bad guys slip into an alley about fifty yards up a wooden walkway. All the money was on the young guy having headed out that way as well. I reached down into my pants pocket and touched the small taser hidden there. Will and I had taken to carrying high-powered tasers on jaunts to strange locales. It was one of those things that wouldn't get you six months in jail if it was noticed going through Customs, but it was a damned effective weapon. I remember the first time we "tried" one. I lost the toss and Will got to tase me first. It was an interesting experience on several levels. When I finally broke away from my friend and quit screeching and flopping around on the floor like headless chicken, we both had learned an important lesson.

Unfortunately, back in the present, the young guy's luck hadn't changed. The alley was a dead end. He turned to face the men. There was fear in his eyes as the larger of the two drew a knife from the small of his back, but there was also defiance. We were still about thirty feet away, approaching quietly, but we weren't going to get there in time.

Suddenly, Will reached down and picked up an empty beer bottle, then started singing and stumbling toward the two men and their prey. "*All alone at the end of the evening...and the bright lights have faded...to blue...*"

I shrugged and joined in on the old Eagles song, stumbling along with Will... *"I was thinkin' 'bout a woman who might have loved me..."*

The whole thing really hammered the momentum the two bad guys had going. They couldn't help themselves. They turned in unison as my friend and I shuffled up to them, taking a quick glance at their prey as well — everyone caught somewhere between the idiocy and the earnestness of the situation.

That was all we needed. Will stepped in and hit the larger fellow on the side of the head with the beer bottle, and I pressed my little taser against the other guy's ribs. He staggered sideways and grabbed his friend's arm, and they both collapsed.

When they hit the ground, both of them had reached the end of the night's entertainment. They weren't going to bother anyone else that evening. Will and I quickly backed away so as to not be part of their "dance."

I looked at the fellow we had just rescued. You would have thought he might have been a little spooked by the situation, but he was smiling.

"Son a bitche!" he said quietly. "Remind me not to get on

the bad side of you two *hombres…*"

"Now tell me that we made the right choice here," I said, "saving your ass."

The guy brought up his hands, palms out. "Oh yeah, man. Oh yeah… It's a long story, but I'ne de good guy here."

One of the fellows on the ground moaned and shivered a little, struggling toward consciousness.

"Come, *mis amigos*," our new acquaintance said hurriedly. "I tell you a story — de good and de bad and de incredible…" He looked at us and his green eyes cleared. "I think you have earned this story. Maybe Dios himself send you my way."

"Time to go, I think," said Will, looking at the guys on the pavement.

Our new friend nodded. He paused and looked at us as if coming to a conclusion. "How about we find another bar and I buy you gringos a drink, eh?"

Twenty minutes later, when we had settled into our seats in the back of another dimly lit room, the young man cocked his head, staring at Will and me.

"Who are you?" he asked. "You not serious surfers. You came to my rescue when you didn't have to. That says much good about you." He paused. "You could have been hurt…or worse…"

Will sighed. "Yeah, we've got a habit of doing stupid things, that's for sure." He offered that half-smile of his. "We're probably adventurers if I had to give it a name. You could say we belong to a small group of people who thrive on unique experiences."

I also offered a slight shrug, adding more than I would have normally but for the evening's margaritas. "We appreciate an odd challenge every once in a while and we're not ashamed of making money as a consequence."

"Lawyers, guns, and money, eh?" said the fellow with a knowing grin, quoting a popular rock song, figuring we were drug smugglers. It was a fairly logical assumption, but it was wrong.

Will smiled. "As well as boats and planes…"

The young man stared at us again, obviously trying to determine whether we were for real. He cocked his head once more. "You got a plane here, now?"

I looked at Will. "Maybe…" I said.

The fellow studied us for a moment longer. "What chu got?"

I exhaled, slightly miffed at the fellow's moxie. "A Cessna 182 long-range amphibian."

Our new acquaintance smiled. "Mmm…perfect." He nodded. "Okay, how about if I trade you a story…for a ride in your *aeroplane?"*

"A story?" I said. *"A story?* It would have to be a really good tale."

"Oohh, it is," he replied. "It is, amigo. You see, I need some help right now, in a…fashion…and I don' have many places to turn." He sighed, then offered a somewhat disarming smile. "Better yet, it might be 'right up your alley,' as you gringos say." He grinned a sort of off-kilter smile. "You know Dios, he moves in strange ways. But you have to pay attention or you can miss the nuances…"

"You could be risking a lot, not knowing anything about us…" I added.

"I know this," our new friend said, holding up an index finger. "You risked your life for a stranger — for no gain." He offered that crooked smile again. "It is like that gringo bandit in the Americano television, you know, the Lone Gringo who has de Indian compadre…"

Will and I looked at each other. We couldn't help but chuckle.

"Yeah," said Will. "The Lone Ranger."

"Si, si, estan el uno!" cried our friend with a smile. *"Si! Es* the one!"

Will looked at me, shook his head incredulously, and

grinned. "Sometimes you just gotta play the part the gods have given you..."

The fellow sighed in an almost thankful fashion. "My name is Diego," he said. "Diego Tarras."

And so, in the back of a grubby little bar in a small surfer town, a young man decided to tell us a story — an unbelievable story on several levels, with a very unique prize being part of the tale. A *very* unique prize...

CHAPTER TWO

Diego moved in, arms on the table in a conspiratorial fashion. He took a breath, glanced at both of us as if making a final decision, and began.

First, he told us about the bar fight over two years ago and the man who had died, mentioning briefly that as a result, Diego had been sentenced to two years in prison. Then he told us about his victim's father and the price he'd put on his head after he got out. He paused and stared at us in that strange manner again. Diego Tarras sighed heavily.

"It was not a good situation. I could barely see my parents — for risking them and me. I was on my own. I am a wanted man — wanted by bad people."

But there was more — a situation beyond belief, like out of a bad fiction novel.

Diego drew a breath. "You ever hear of de island of Coiba, thirty miles off the coast of Panama?"

I hesitated for a moment. The name was somewhat familiar, but I wasn't sure. But Will, our group's historian and part-time professor, nodded his head enthusiastically.

"Yeah, man, I've heard of it. You bet I've heard of it." He pulled in closer. "From what I've read, stepping onto Coiba is like stepping back in time a thousand years. The island was separated from continental Panama somewhere around 12,000 to 18,000 years ago, when sea levels on the planet rose. But now it sits about thirty miles west of the mainland of Panama. They say the flora and fauna became isolated from mainland populations and took on unique appearances and behaviors considerably different from their counterparts in Central America."

Will was on one of his rolls. I wasn't getting in the way.

"There are over a thousand plant species and wild, robust forests filled with strange plants and animals — the red-haired stepchildren of environmental ecology," my buddy continued. "But even beyond that, they say there is a different...*feeling*...to much of the stuff there. In particular, the plant life. Scientists and botanists agree there is a robustness to the plant growth — a strength, variety, and durability you don't find in other parts of the Caribbean. Or anywhere, for that matter."

Our new friend nodded vigorously. "*Si! Si!* De island has plants that are jus' impossible to believe unless you see them — like something out of an Americano science-fiction movie. Like...if de gringo, Cameron, an' that Spielberg gringo get together and do acid, eh?"

I couldn't help but grin. "Very interesting," I said, a little more curious now.

Will became slightly sober then, and his face darkened. "But Coiba Island is a prison now, if I'm not mistaken. Has been for almost a hundred years. It's been run by some of the most notorious dictators in the history of Panama. It's a penal colony that has held some of Panama's most dangerous criminals and political prisoners."

Will took a breath and ran his hand through his long blond hair, his blue eyes coming alive with the tale. "Unlike most penitentiaries where the criminals are housed within large, fortress-like facilities, on Coiba, most of the prisoners are scattered across the island, living in makeshift camps and forced to create their own shelters from natural surroundings. It is the guards and officials who live in the rock fortress/penitentiary at the northern end of the island with special facilities for the most dangerous or politically important inmates, protected from the island's prisoner-inhabitants by stone walls." Will held up a finger. "In its later days, under Panama's brutal dictatorships of Omar Torrijos and Manuel Noriega, the prison and its surrounding penal colony have contained as many as 3,000 inmates. Those who were sent to Coiba during the reigns of Torrijos and Noriega were known as *los desaparecidos*, or *the disappeared.* Hundreds of prisoners were buried in unmarked graves or dismembered and thrown to the sharks."

Will recognized the incredulousness in my eyes and shrugged. "I know it all sounds a little far-fetched, but it's true! I first found out about this place through the Encyclopedia Britannica, then I researched it through my Miami library companion. It's common information, regardless of how uncommon it sounds."

Over the last few years, Will had made a connection with the lady who oversaw the historical department in Miami's largest library. She was older but not unattractive. A "cougar" was the term my friend used in a somewhat endearing fashion. It involved a couple of dinners and a night or two of "more intimate entertainment" on occasion, but it bought my friend unfettered historical investigation at her library.

Will paused again, and in the silence, Diego exhaled and suddenly spoke quietly from bitter memory, his face taut, as if he had to get something out.

"I was a prisoner on de island of Coiba for thirteen hellish months," Diego said almost in a whisper, his green eyes distant in recall. "No communication with anyone off de island in that time." He sighed. "My family think I am dead. At first, I was held in the stone prison. Truly a hell on earth, amigos — a crudely built rock fortress where Panama's political prisoners stayed and where people like myself, who had injured the government in some fashion, were made to pay." He exhaled again, the recollection clouding his eyes. "People tortured… executed…every day..." He looked up at us. "The electricity worked only occasionally, de food was barely edible and never enough, and you fought the rats for it. I lose thirty pounds in the first three months!"

Diego paused and drew a shaky breath. I could tell the memories were psychologically brutal.

"There were attempts to try to rescue prisoners from the stone prison, but almost no successes. Fifteen-foot walls made from natural stone and lava rock, laced with rolls of razor wire on top… Inside there were barracks made of the same stone with small barred windows for what little ventilation was allowed." He paused again, his eyes filled with recollection and pain. "Prisoners who displeased the guards or de authorities in any fashion often had their windows closed off — left to bake in the tropical ovens called cells. At night, as the moon and the clouds cast shadows over hell on earth, you could hear them crying hoarsely, some trying to drink their tears…"

Diego came back to the present with a sigh.

"Then, finally, when they felt they had punished me enough, or they realized I hadn't died, they push me out de big doors of the fortress to live off the land — or jungle, actually — for the remainder of my sentence." He shook his head. "You alone had to remember the day your sentence was over and appear at the gate of de rock fortress then. No one checked for you, no one came for you… But being free from the prison meant nothing. Coiba was an island of lush flora and fauna and most of de prisoners lived outside de fortress walls — to fend for themselves in hellish communes." He chuckled mirthlessly. "What look like a gift was just another version of hell." He paused again and brought up his arms. "Can you imagine being forced into a jungle wilderness, full of savage men who live in tribes of sorts — brutal camps. Men absolutely devoid of morals or honor. And no one being able to escape the island, which is surrounded by terrible sea currents, with a dozen varieties of sharks, poison jellyfish, and sea-going crocodiles along the shoreline and rivers…and all this patrolled by government boats with the closest land an impossible thirty miles away." He exhaled hard again. "This was my life for the second year…"

There was really no appropriate reply on our part. We were quiet as, once again, Diego paused and took a few breaths. The recollection was bitterly hard.

"I live in hell for that last year, constantly challenged by man and beast — spiders the size of dinner plates, poison snakes, and big cats — an' the monkeys! Huge howler monkeys barking continuously in the jungle. I was never certain of survival past the sunrise. I believe the only reason anyone survive those conditions was all the incredible fruits and vegetables, and strange animals on the island. It was like de Garden of Eden run by the devil."

His eyes took on a faraway glint.

"But there was one other thing about that island. The ruins…ruins of de ancient culture that existed, with knowledge and pride, long before even de conquistadores."

There was something in this dissertation that was personal, but Diego wasn't ready to release it. He continued, eyes still distant. "Sometimes, when I thought I was safe, I would move through de long-dead, jungle-absorbed ruins — ancient walls covered with strange runes that moved up and melted into de sandstone, and granite cliffs shrouded by vine and leaf…" He paused and the light in his eyes came on again. "Places where there was no determining where de ancient walls stopped and de hills and vines took over, shrouding the dead village and the lost secrets."

I felt as if the guy was close to telling us something, but he just wasn't quite ready.

"He's right," said Will quietly. "The island has an interesting history. It was home to the indigenous Coiba Cacique people until the mid-1500s, when the Spanish conquistadors 'discovered' those folks, and promptly went about killing, enslaving, and gradually annihilating them. When there was nothing left to take or kill, the Spanish left."

We sat there quietly for a few moments, then Will picked up one last time.

"Given its reputation — the island and the prison and the fact that it isn't easily reached from the mainland — the place has been pretty much avoided by everyone, and it's totally undeveloped. I'm told it's like a time capsule." He held up a finger. "But I remember those who explored that area said it was as if the island had been 'cared for by the gods.'" Then he turned to our new friend, and with that rare intuitiveness of his, Will asked, "But there's more, isn't there? There's still something you're not saying. Something you're not telling us. Or we wouldn't be here now. You would have already gone your way and you wouldn't need an airplane..."

Diego stared at Will for a moment and their eyes held, then he sighed heavily and broke away, looking down at the table. *"Si, mi* intuitive gringo. There is more." He exhaled again, and then began to tell the story buried inside him. The one he could barely believe himself. A remarkable tale about a hidden entrance in the ruins of a long-lost Cacique Indian temple, a strange, weighted stone door that led to a small room in a granite hillside, and "the Blood of the Gods."

"It was not so much a cave..." Diego began to explain.

"Oohh, Jesus," Will hissed. "Not another cave! Please! After that freaking Venezuela gig, I've had all the caves I want for a lifetime." He held out his hands. "Is there a cliff as well?" He looked at me. "You know how much I like cliffs."

I waved my buddy down and Diego continued, partly here, partly there. "They call it 'the 'Blood of the Gods,'" he said in an almost reverent whisper. "And I suppose it could be, who knows? But it is there, vaguely mentioned in de ancient chronicles of the Cacique...the Blood of the Gods... In the pre-Columbian archives provided by Spain, in the Panamanian city of Santiago..." He sighed softly. "I checked. It was de first thing I do when I got out of prison."

Then our friend suddenly switched courses. His eyes cleared and he stared at us again with clarity and purpose. "And now I suppose you want to know what it is I found, eh, amigos?"

"Yep," muttered Will. "Now would be a good time."

CHAPTER THREE

"*Si*, now is a good time," Diego agreed. He looked around the bar. "But we need to take a walk. Too many eyes and ears here."

So we went out and strolled along the moonlit beach, ending up by the remains of a battered lifeguard station. Diego exhaled heavily and turned to Will and me.

"You know now about how unusual de island of Coiba is with all the strange, vibrant flora and extraordinary growth, but you don' know *why*. Nobody knows why. Not even the botanists and the scientists who have studied it know why." He looked at us and offered a slight smile tempered with a touch of hesitation. "I might be de only person in the world who knows..." Again he offered that odd smile of his. "It is a secret that could change the earth. It is a secret worth millions of dollars. Millions! The Blood of the Gods, amigos — the Blood of the Gods. That's the secret that lies hidden in de walls of the old Cacique ruins, and I accidentally stumbled onto it."

He shrugged, taking down the intensity a notch. "The problem is, I know what and where, but I don' have de means to go back into that hellish island, get what waits there, and get back out alive." He held out his hands, palms up. "Oh, I might get lucky and get in and out, maybe. But with de right means, I could increase the odds of success." He looked at us. "You have the means and I believe the character to succeed at this. And truthfully, the wealth is so great from this...thing...that I am willing to take less and live to tell about it, eh?"

Will took a breath and straightened up. He glanced at me.

I nodded. "Okay," I said. "You've got our attention. So...

what's the gig about?"

Our new friend stared at us for a moment, making that final, very difficult decision. Then he sighed again and began.

"While I was living in de interior of Coiba Island, I had been 'accepted' by one of the small camps, but it was a horrible situation. They were barely men anymore. More like animals, living in makeshift palm huts, cooking animals over open fires, and often brutalizing each other for the smallest of reasons." He let out a shaky breath. "I tried to stay gone as much as possible. I would explore the island for days at a time. There were many ruins of de early Cacique Indians, and they were fascinating, but in my wanderings, I began to notice something else. In most places, the language that was etched on shattered walls here and there carried the crudeness of an early people — primitive in structure. But I find a place or two that were different. The writing in them was not primitive — it was flowing and it seemed almost...how you say...*elegant*." He hesitated and drew a breath. "So...one day I find this place, what seem like a natural slit in a wall of rock. I slip in because I am a curious fool. The entrance leads into an almost round room. The walls inside this place I find — maybe it was a small temple of some sort — were smooth, almost as if dey had been heated and the rock had been...melted." He exhaled. "Very unusual. And there was a place with writing on the wall — very strange writing. Like nothing I have ever seen before — not Indian." Diego paused again. "I don' know any of this for sure, but it seem like two cultures — one, a little primitive, maybe permanent, and one more advanced, dey touch briefly. Eh?"

I looked at Will and his eyes spoke. We'd heard this tune before, in Venezuela. The coincidence was remarkable, even for us. I couldn't help but hear Rufus in my head, *"Chance, flukes, luck...be da dice of da gods..."*

Diego drew another breath. "But there was one thing more that confuse me most. As I look around, I find something. There is a stone door, so artfully made that almost no seam could be seen. I wouldn't have noticed. But I am inside the first cave, I lean against a wall, and maybe I touch something, and the door slide open next to me." He shrugged. "As I said, I am a curious fool, so slowly I go in. Inside there is a small room with a skeleton. A tall skeleton with an odd-shaped skull, sitting against the wall, as if de fellow had decided to rest. Who knows? But when I look close, through the deteriorated film of the robe-like garment it had on, I see some bones are broken — ribs, an arm, and there is a fracture in the skull. It is obvious this strange person have a serious accident of some sort."

Diego came back to us, eye to eye now. "But above de skeleton, carved into the wall, was a shelf. On the shelf is three glass-like containers, about the size of large whiskey flasks, maybe ten or twelve ounces, but the glass was dark, like the old rum bottles of de ancient pirates."

Will glanced at me and I caught the message in his eyes. *The dark glass was used so that sunlight wouldn't affect the quality of the contents. Interesting...*

My partner smiled and I saw that familiar, hungry gleam in his eyes. This was definitely turning into a tale of some interest.

"So," continued Diego, "naturally, I decide to take one of the bottles. I think maybe they are ancient liquor or medicine. Who knows? I leave the cave and the stone door closes behind me without a sound — without barely a single sign of it being there. So, now I have this bottle of...*something*. I drift over to a pool by a little freshwater creek and sit down to think about what has happened. Around the pool is some bushes and flowers, and a few small trees, some with fruit — the same terrain along the creek as it wanders down, away from de high ground and toward de shore of the island."

Our friend took a breath and shrugged. "Fortunately, I decide not to taste or touch this liquid. Dios! Who knows what this might be, eh? But I'm still very curious, so I open the bottle and look at it. I notice now that the bottle has an engraving of what looks like a fruit on de front — another strange thing. I pour a little in the cap and smell it. Not much smell, maybe a little bitter… It appears a dark red, like blood, with just about the same thickness. I shrug and throw the capful of liquid into the water at the edge of the shore. There is no apparent value I can see, and I am no going to taste it — that is for sure. So, I put the cap back on, then put the bottle in my pocket. But it is now pretty late, so I decide to stay for the night in the cave of de bottles." He grinned slightly. "I not so happy about the skeleton on de floor, but Dios, he was there before me, eh?"

"This is going somewhere pretty quick, I hope," muttered Will.

"Yeah, yeah, it's goin' somewhere," said Diego. "Trust me." He drew a breath. "So, next day I leave the area, sort of following the creek inland, moving back toward the campsite of dangerous idiots and the prison fortress. But by sunset, I am making camp and I realize I have lost my knife — I maybe lose it or leave it at my camp by the cave." He paused and looked at us, and his eyes narrowed. "A knife is a very important thing on that island. That knife I take from a man who tried to kill me."

The inference was ugly.

Diego continued. "So, I have to go back. I sleep that night in a tree, and at dawn, I start." He paused again. "This is where the story get interesting."

"Good…" grumbled Will. "I'm looking forward to that."

"By de afternoon, I am hiking along the little creek, winding my way back, when I begin to notice something. All the plants, flowers, even de damn trees along the stream seem to be…more healthy now. De wild mangos and papayas, de guayabas, even the wild bananas, they have changed slightly." He shook his head, wrapped in the memory and disbelief. "I think maybe it's my imagination, so I stop several times to explore this thing that has happened. I am not making good time in this process, so I camp for another night." Our friend took a breath and smiled. "There is nothing to be in a hurry about on that island. So, I sleep that night and begin again, and all the while, everything around the little creek seems to be getting more...*healthy*. It is very strange, I tell you. The next day, when I make it back to the pool in the creek where I toss the liquid, I know it is not my imagination. Everything — all de flora, as you say — around that area is fuller, some things are even bigger." He looked at us and shrugged. "It seem impossible but it is true. And it gets better. I realize something is going on here, something I don' understand, and I don' want to take this back to the dangerous *idiotas* in the villages of the damned or de prison fortress. So, I stay where I am. I make a camp, and for the last month of my sentence, I stay there, experimenting with de magic juice." His eyes became serious. "De results were amazing and I think I know now why de island of Coiba is considered a 'miracle island' in exotic plants, flowers, and fruits." He drew another breath. "I believe maybe it was an experimental place for developing plants, fruits, and vegetables...maybe for this planet. Maybe by some special ancients or some very distant people...perhaps thousands of years ago." Diego sighed.

Will nodded. "Maybe...assisted evolution?"

"I think Coiba maybe could have been a 'staging base,'" Diego whispered, "to help make survival more comfortable in de long process of evolution...here and there..." He sighed again. "I know it is bizarre...but seeing is believing in this place."

I cocked my head, really curious now. "So, you think maybe this juice apparently ramps up the metabolism of flora of all sorts? Maybe an important element in the preparation of the nest called Earth, huh?"

Will eased back a little and glanced at me, eyebrows up in question. Then he turned back to Diego. "That's quite a stretch, amigo — quite a tale. So, what you're telling us is you may have found a magic elixir for growing things quickly — a working alchemy for the empowerment of flora, cutting growth time by maybe eighty, ninety percent while increasing quality?" He paused and looked at our new buddy, somewhat interested but definitely skeptical. "Terraforming or terraformation — that's what it's called in scientific circles. Even though it hasn't been managed to any great degree yet that I know of." He took a breath. "So, at this point, I'm assuming that A, you have some of this juice, and B, you're willing to offer a demonstration forthwith. Because otherwise, I go back to my original assumption — which is, truthfully, at this point, I think you're full of shit."

Diego smiled. "*Si* — yes to both of your expectancies."

He reached into his shirt and pulled out a thin leather thong. At the end of it was tied a small brown bottle with a black twist-off lid — the kind cocaine fans use. He held it out to us.

"This is all I have now. The rest is still on the island. I returned the bottle I had opened to the cave. I had no way to get it off Coiba when I was freed and returned to Panama." He nervously pushed back his long, dark hair with the fingers of one hand. "They search you almost as thoroughly when you go out as when you arrive. I could only bring out what I could hide in the most…" He paused. "…discreet places."

It was pretty clear. We didn't need a picture. We didn't *want* a picture.

"But I need to go back to de island now," Diego said. "To get the remaining bottles…" Again he stopped. "I don' need to explain to you how much something like this is worth. If it can be reproduced, it is a world changer."

Will looked at our new acquaintance. "Again, why us? Why a couple of adventurers? Why didn't you take this to the Panamanian Department of Agriculture?"

Diego stared at him. "Because this is Central America, amigo, not Texas. I would be dead two days after they confirmed what I have. An unfortunate 'accident' and someone 'official' would be filing a patent. And besides, like I said earlier, you are adventurers by nature and you have de amphibian plane, which will be necessary to get into and out of de island." He offered a grin. "Truly timing made by the gods."

Will shrugged. "Yeah, you're probably right. But to tell you the truth, I don't think your survival would be that different in the States. Greed is greed. To survive, you'd have to quietly form an independent company, do your testing secretly, file your patents, then announce what you have. But first, buddy, before you talk me into flying to a prison island for a bottle of magic juice, I'm gonna have to see the magic work. The proof is in the pudding."

Diego nodded. *"Si,* it is. So be it. We will meet in the little park at the end of town. Cortez Public Park. Ten in the morning, by the fountain." He paused. "Bring a plant or a small tree that you would like to see become more...healthy."

When all was said and done and Diego had gone his way, Will and I sat watching the sun come up from the porch of our little villa. I couldn't help but think of our old Rastaman buddy, Rufus, who had been known to say... *"You think it's luck or fate or dat you be something special. But no, mon, no... It just be de gods... Dey be getting bored. So dey make some circumstance for a little entertainment. You be just a couple dangling puppets."*

Too true, mon. Too true...

■ ■ ■

It had been over six months since our last incredible adventure in South America — the pursuit of a crystal skull that led to an incredible maze of events and characters, then climaxed with an airplane crash that buried a couple of Smithsonian Institute bad guys and that incredible skull in six thousand feet of water off the coast of Venezuela. Maybe the gods of adventure thought that was enough of a break for us. Nonetheless, here we were, back in the game of adventure via no real effort or fault of our own.

My friend sighed, still staring at the brilliant sunrise, and I could see those intellectual wheels turning in his head. He spoke without looking at me.

"Aside from oxygen and water, any new/early species has to have a consistent supply of food. A hunter-gatherer society can only go so far — it is constantly moving, never establishing a culture, always dependent on tomorrow's hunt. There had to be someone or something that jump-started that type of society into a genuine, established, flourishing culture in various places. Maybe, just maybe, this lucky break came from the stars and was kindly dropped into the laps of primitive man here and there because he just couldn't seem to get his act together enough as a hunter-gatherer. More animals were eating him than vice versa. Something had to give if this new creature on the evolutionary block was going to survive. It was a jungle out there, literally…"

Will looked at me. "Let's go have breakfast, then buy a big plant or a small tree. We've got a couple hours to kill before we get the magic juice."

A short time later, while we sat at a table on the patio of a little restaurant, Will took a sip of his coffee. "If you remember, during our last adventure into Venezuela, we came to realize the possibility of spiritually enlightened intergalactic travelers. What if these or similar folks perfected an easily dispensable, highly concentrated formula of 'magic juice' which, when mixed with water, seriously enhanced the growth of essential flora — fruit trees, field grains, and vegetables — and they shared it. Sort of like intergalactic, spiritually connected Johnny Appleseeds."

I held up a hand. "If that were the case, my guess would be these 'Appleseeders' wouldn't have provided an unlimited supply of this miracle juice. They would have only offered enough for a season or two, or a little for an agricultural emergency down the road, then went on their way." I paused. "I remember someone of importance saying, 'For a society to be successful long-term, it can never be dependent on any single thing for survival.'"

"Tell that to this new generation addicted to and obsessed with the electronic boxes they stare at and talk into incessantly,"

Will muttered.

There was a pause, then Will picked up again.

"Terraformation… A splash of special magic juice, possibly distributed on crops here and there by the benevolent folks from somewhere…and shazam! Inside one season you've got veggies and fruit trees sprouting everywhere and survival for your species is in sight."

"I know that for the conventionally religious, this 'folks from another place faraway' is still a huge gulp," I added. "But if you simply look at this as a possibility, it is one of the most natural ways for intelligent life on this planet, and perhaps other planets, to have had a chance. To have been gifted survival by those who understood it better."

"And when it comes to this terraformation/magic water thing, think about the number of tales and legends that relate stories of water carrying extraordinary powers in our combined histories," Will said. "For instance, the ancient tales of Shambala, the mythical kingdom and its special waters, taken from Tibetan Buddhist tradition. Or the Incas, with their dedication to the collection and ceremonial use of the special 'tears of the gods.' Or the holy liquids and 'water gods' found in so many of India's rituals." He paused and looked at me. "Then, of course, there's Christianity, with its baptismal dunks and splashes, and holy wines and waters right and left. Where did the concept of all these magic waters come from, do you suppose?"

"Yeah, I know, I know," I said, bringing up a hand. "Lord, when you look up at the stars on a clear, cloudless night and consider the vast, infinite panorama of solar systems — it gives you pause. It allows you to believe in possibilities. I'm not talking about anyone setting aside their *faith* here. I'm just saying maybe suspend your *religion* for a moment — because the two are not necessarily the same."

"Religion always demands," Will whispered. "But faith sweeps in softly and assures."

I looked at my buddy. "That's beautiful, man, and true."

Will offered that crooked smile. "I have my moments," he said. "Now, back to the sixty-four-dollar question. What would happen if a couple of clever fellows actually got hold of a container or two of this magic-grow juice? What would that be worth on the open market?"

"I would think a person could get himself very rich or very dead," I replied with a cautious shrug. "Depending on how the dice fell."

CHAPTER FOUR

We stopped at a nursery and bought a small, four-foot-tall rubber tree in a galvanized tub of soil — old enough and strong enough to endure common challenges but not so big that we had to rent a pickup to carry it around. We left it in the villa, then headed over to the park.

Diego was waiting for us on a bench near a statue of Panama's once president for life, Manuel Noriega. At his side, on the ground, was an empty glass gallon jug. We did a brief greeting thing, then got down to business.

After a few admonitions and promises, Diego looked around cautiously, then pulled the vial out from underneath his shirt and slipped the leather thong off his neck. He removed the lid from the empty jug, then removed the screw top from the tiny brown bottle. "I am doing this here, risking this, because I need you to be certain that there is no trickery on my part. One or two drops in a gallon of water," he said as he turned up the tiny bottle and slowly allowed two drops to slip into thc container. He sighed and gave it an extra shot or two, then looked up. "Go," he said, handing the jug to Will. "Fill it with water from de faucet over there."

My partner obeyed like a well-trained poodle.

When Will returned, our new friend stared at us. "It is ready now. Go — put the water on your plant or tree that you have. It needs twenty-four hours at least. That will not give you dynamic results in that time but it will make my point, I am sure." He sighed. It sounded almost desperate. "I gave it a little extra." He shrugged. "Maybe too much..." Then he paused and exhaled. "But do not wait beyond tomorrow morning to get back to me.

Every moment I stay in Panama I risk being killed for money. We need to leave soon."

Our friend's personality had taken on a decidedly serious nature. Not so easy-breezy now.

"Three or four drops is too much, huh?" muttered Will. "I feel like an actor in a bad sci-fi movie."

"Meet me here tomorrow at noon," said Diego. "By then, you will..." He paused. "...understand. And have your *aeroplane* ready to go."

Will and I glanced at each other. *The son of a bitch seemed awfully confident.*

Will turned to Diego. "How about this, amigo. Why don't you come with us now and we'll get you a room where we're staying — El Castile. That way we're all together if we need to get out in a hurry. Okay*?"*

Our new partner in moderate crimes thought about it for a moment, then nodded. "This is probably a good plan. I go get my things and meet you in an hour. *Bueno*...amigos."

Then he was gone and we were left with the sunshine, General Noriega, and a gallon of magic juice.

"How in the hell do we get into these things?" grumbled Will, holding our precious cargo. "All I wanted was to do a little surfing and chase a beach bunny or two. Now here I am staring into some sort of mysterious Stephen King song and dance about voodoo plant juice, dangerous islands, and people wanting to kill people, all in about twenty-four hours!" He threw up his arms. "How does this happen? Huh?"

I shook my head. "It's pretty bizarre, I gotta admit. But hang in there, Tonto. I think it's gonna get even more interesting."

Will held up a forefinger and shook it at me. "No. Let's get this straight now, from the beginning. Me, the Lone Ranger. You, Tonto."

■ ■ ■

Teta Takos was watching all this from a bench on the other side of the park. It was a curious thing — the two gringos and this *hermano* with a glass jug, and the little cocaine bottle around his neck. He carefully gives the jug a couple of drops, then gives it back to them. Yes...this was a curious thing.

Takos liked to think of himself as a man of opportunity instead of the scrawny, lowlife thief and part-time drug dealer that he actually was. But the whole affair with the *Americanos* seemed strange, even for him... So strange it made his glass eye go wonky. Whenever he got excited, that damn crazy glass eye would slide sideways, into the corner of its socket, as if it was excited by something near his ear. It was very disconcerting to all concerned, especially Teta. Nonetheless, he had some time to kill, so he decided to follow the gringos on his scooter. The Central American con man shrugged. Why not? He had nothing to lose. Even more curious was the fact that the Latin with them looked an awful lot like the parolee who had a street price on his head from the circuit judge. Five hundred balboas — dead or...dead. *Alive* was not an option.

Teta was not a large man and he was thin as well, with long, somewhat frizzy hair and "Indian-black" eyes. He wasn't really big on violence, especially if it could bleed over onto him. But he had caught enough of the conversation in the park to realize that these people were up to something.

■ ■ ■

Will and I returned to our room and while we waited for Diego to show up, we took our new tree out onto the small balcony where it could get some sun. Then, without too much ceremony, I dumped the gallon of specially seasoned water into the dirt.

Will looked at me. "Well, either the dam is going to hold or it isn't."

I nodded. "Amen, brother."

From the parking lot, Teta watched the two gringos carefully position the potted tree in the sunlight on the porch, then dump a gallon of water on it.

He shrugged. "These gringos are very strange people," he whispered to himself.

A half-hour after we had "fed" our tree, Diego showed up. We decided to grab some lunch, then head over to the airport and make sure the bills were paid and our airplane was primed and ready to roll. We had learned from past experience that on occasion, we did stupid things that required quick exits.

The rest of the day was fairly uneventful. My buddy and I did a little sightseeing and caught a few waves while Diego watched from the beach — wearing dark sunglasses and a big hat. He had explained again that this magic juice thing was at the very least a twenty-four-hour affair for any results, but he also added once more that he had hit that little rubber tree "a little on the hard side" with the juice.

Neither of us really disbelieved our new friend (we were, by nature, children of the bizarre) but the whole thing — the story of the cave, the skeleton, the magic juice, the plants, the terrible island with all the crazy people on it, and our new acquaintance with a price on his head — was just so preposterous, it seemed almost above our level of coincidental entertainment.

■ ■ ■

During this time, Teta spoke with one of his street acquaintances and managed to get a photo of the man the judge wanted dead. He drove to the hotel entrance and waited on a bench under a mahogany tree across the street. He was not necessarily a patient man but he had nothing else to do and nowhere else to go, and five hundred balboas was a lot of money. It made his crazy eye go wonky just thinking about it.

Later that day, the gringos came back with their friend. Teta, sitting on the city bus bench by the hotel, stared at the fellow, then quickly studied the photo. *Si! Si! No question! It is him. Five hundred balboas! Caramba! The gods are smiling!* He stuffed the paper into his pocket and casually rose, then walked away, trying to get his crazy eye back in place.

■ ■ ■

The good news was, the weather was holding over the Caribbean and we could get out in the morning without a problem. The bad news was a man named Señor Mateo Preces, who wanted payment for his dead son.

The remainder of our evening was filled with cautious optimism. I ordered dinner for the three of us to be delivered to our room, where Diego joined us. No more going out, no risk-taking. We were headed for the finish line.

I brought out my aeronautical map and did some figuring. It was about 950 miles from our local airport here to Cancun, Mexico, which was about a seven-hour run. We'd spend the night in Cancun and be out at a reasonable time the following morning. I figured if we were in the air by nine a.m., we could pack that last 400 miles to Key West into three hours, no problem. If we could just get out tomorrow without incident...

It had been a fast couple of days without much sleep, so we opted for nightcaps in our room, then Diego bid us good night and headed for his room. Before bed, Will and I went out and looked at our little tree. It had been about eight hours since I had given it the magic juice. I figured that would be long enough for maybe a little change if this stuff was as good as Diego said. I wasn't disappointed.

The tiny rubber tree now definitely had more of a sense of robustness to it. The leaves were fuller and darker, and I was certain I saw tiny nubs of growth that represented new branches — not a lot, but there was a notable change. I mean, it wasn't something that would make me jump up and down, but it had only been a few hours so it was pretty amazing.

Will and I retired, somewhat encouraged. But when we awoke eight hours later, there was a bit of a different situation…

Actually, it was Will who woke me. "Hey, man," he said, shaking my shoulder. "You gotta get up."

I rose with a start, trying to clear my eyes, concerned by the anxiousness in his voice. "What's wrong?" I mumbled.

"Nothing's wrong," said my friend, standing next to me. "I just wanted you to get up and have some coffee with me, out on the balcony. We're burning daylight."

"Okay, okay," I muttered, sliding back the covers and reaching for my jeans.

A couple of minutes later, I stumbled into the kitchen and grabbed a cup of coffee. Will was out on the balcony taking in the sunrise, so I headed in that direction. The curtains to the balcony were drawn, but the sliding doors were open and I could feel the breeze. I slid back the curtains, stepped out, and gasped.

Will was standing by the railing, a cup of coffee in one hand and a Cheshire Cat smile spread across his face. Our little rubber tree was still where we'd left it, in the center of the balcony. But…there was a whole lot more tree now. It had grown over a foot in height. Some of the branches, half a size larger than they were last night, were hungrily reaching for the railing and the new sunlight. I was waiting for the damned thing to growl! It was extraordinary and spooky at the same time. (*Overnight — over freaking night!)*

There was no question now that our friend — that *we* — clearly possessed something of serious value. I wasn't sure if the metabolism of a small tree like that could support a growth rate like we were seeing and not burn out, but for right now, I was seriously impressed.

I turned to Will. "Get dressed and packed. I'll go wake Diego. We're getting out of here. *Now.*"

A half-hour later, we were in our rental car and headed back toward the small local airport. We took our still-growing rubber tree and dumped it in the jungle along the road outside of town.

No use advertising a million-dollar idea.

Everything was looking pretty good…but then we should have remembered what Rufus always said. *"Da gods, dey love surprises."*

As we pulled up at the small Santa Catalina airport FBO and got out of our rental, a guy standing by the runway fence studied us, then looked at the photo he had. He stared at Diego once more, then brought up one of the newer cell phones.

I did my preflight, then we settled up with the FBO manager. Once both of these things were complete, we were escorted into the small Customs office, where our few bags were checked and our passports were verified. Fortunately, Diego had possessed the presence of mind to get his passport when he had visited his parents recently.

We were just finishing when I noticed two custom black Lincoln Town Cars coming down the road toward us. Black Lincoln Town Cars always make me nervous, no matter what country I'm in. They are a conveyance of the privileged, the official, and often the dangerous, regardless of where you are.

I looked at Will and Diego. Their eyes offered the same message. *Get the hell out of Dodge — now…*

"Time to go," I hissed, nodding at the approaching company.

We headed across the tarmac in a rush, and had just made the plane as the people in the Lincolns began to pull up at the FBO and exit their vehicles. There was an older guy with gray hair, dignified, nice suit, but not happy at all. A guy that looked like a shaved gorilla got the door for him. The older man's eyes were narrowing on us before he'd taken a dozen steps. Exiting behind him in the other car were four more well-dressed goons with bulges under their coats, and a little guy that seemed totally out of place. The big boys were already reaching for the bulges.

Everyone had already found a seat in the Cessna (it's amazing how fear expedites things). I was turning the key and the engine was responding as the gorillas in the nice clothes started running in our direction, guns coming up. As I slammed the throttle forward, I could hear the familiar "pop" of weaponry. The glass behind my head suddenly fractured with a bang. I'll admit I might have screamed then, in between trying to sound "routine" to the tower as they directed me to our runway. There were several more pops as the aluminum hull took hits, but in moments, we were out of range. I swung around at the threshold of the runway, got clearance for takeoff, and we were nothing but thin air and history a minute later.

After a brief conversation with the police and the exchange of a few balboas, Señor Preces and his people drove away unscathed. They left Teta standing there, alone...but not shot. Which was a pretty good deal as far as Teta was concerned.

■ ■ ■

Will managed to duct tape the gunshot window. The other rounds that struck the hull of the plane apparently didn't do any major damage. So, once again, we were on our way out of one adventure and into a new one in hopes that the "entertaining the gods" thing would continue to apply to present company.

I was reminded of one other expression by Rufus: *"It don' be da destination dat matters so much, mon, but da experience of getting dere."*

CHAPTER FIVE

By the time we reached Key West the following day, things were settling down some — or just ramping up, depending on the way you looked at it. I would have normally flown the floatplane back to my canal home on Big Pine. But instead, after clearing Customs, we dropped it off at the airport hangar that our group (informally known as the Hole in the Coral Wall Gang) shared. My bird would need some repairs before we began seriously moving toward a trip back to Panama. There were a few bullet holes…

Cody and Travis, our two other significant members, both owned aircraft as well, and they kept them at the same hangar. They had spent a good deal of time in the military — Vietnam, mostly — Cody in spotter planes and Special Ops, and Travis in his legendary helicopters and his incredible rescue missions. Travis — six feet plus, heavily muscled, dark hair, green eyes — went in where no one else would and he brought the boys back. Both he and Cody had boxes of medals they never talked about and reputations they never mentioned, but I never saw either of them buy their own drinks in any military bar. Watching Travis go into a U.S. base bar was like watching a John Wayne movie — the silence for a moment, then the casual pointing and whispering, then the soldiers, both enlisted men and officers, going over just to shake his hand…and the bartender stopping by to humbly tell him that his money was no good there.

Cody Joe, also a survivor of the sweat and blood of Southeast Asian jungles, mission after mission — a connoisseur of good beer and fine women, and a man with the same resilience and history as his friend — resided on a little forty-five-foot Morgan sailboat anchored in Key West Harbor. Mostly now he was a blond-haired, blue-eyed Casanova — a free spirit and a very hard character to tie to a single cleat, but a damned good man to have at your side in a sticky situation.

And there was Crazy Eddie, owner of one of Key West's more popular bars and the senior member of our gang, who kept his Grumman Goose parked outside the hangar. Eddie came by his reputation honestly. I was pretty sure he was genuinely crazy. Just his image was something out of *Adventure Magazine* — longish brown hair, a bushy mustache, and a patch over one eye. Right out of a pirate or an Old West movie. His favorite possession in the world was a ball cap Jimmy Buffett had given him after a wild night on the town. Eddie was sort of the civilian, smaller version of Travis, with a penchant for shiny old things and pretty young things. He was the only person I knew who could actually scare Travis and Cody in an airplane.

I guess we were all pretty much fond of items that defied gravity. When I thought about it, I realized that we were constantly defying things…odds, safety, regulations, natural laws, death, and life…

There were, however, a couple of new additions to the team about whom I had seriously mixed feelings.

It was a most interesting story regarding those two, Tax and Jing. Well over twenty years ago in the Keys, both Will and I fell in love with the same woman — the randy and beautiful Banyan McDaniel. She couldn't make up her mind with us, so she sort of bounced back and forth for a while. In one of those nearly impossible situations (studied mostly in college biology), both my friend and I managed to impregnate her, resulting in non-identical twins. Long before anyone knew this had happened, Banyan left us for a conga player in some sort of Caribbean marimba band and disappeared into the sunset. Then, twenty years later, we ran into Tax and Jing at a bar in New Orleans. We were struck by how much they looked like us, and when we started trading histories, the lights came on. Shortly after that, we contacted their mother in Barbados and she confirmed our "relationship."

While it was a mind-blowing situation, we soon discovered that we all felt a natural empathy for each other that developed into a family relationship. We discovered that those two rascals carried the same affinity for adventure as Will and me. Tax, my son, was twenty-five years old with sun-bleached, shoulder-length hair, inquisitive hazel eyes, and a capable-looking build. His life experiences included a background in street-style martial arts, sailing, a pilot's license, and when it came to anyone screwing around with his sister, the attitude of a pit bull.

Jing, Will's daughter, was just remarkable. She was beautiful, capable, and at times, purely comfortable with being dangerous. At maybe five foot seven or eight, with blue eyes, a nice figure, and shoulder-length blond hair, she was accustomed to second looks. But it was after you got to know her that she really turned your head. Jing had an osprey, a huge sea hawk that she had raised from a fledgling, and there was a bond between them that was uncanny at best, and on occasion, just plain freaky. Her independence and her connection with nature were legendary, and there were times when she and her hawk would just disappear for days at a time. She called her disappearances "forays into the past and present."

Jing had long been a student of ancient history, researching races like the Egyptians, the Mesopotamians, and the mystic Sumerians, studying the powers of conjuring, insight, and "communication with creatures of the field and sky." At first, I just considered it a passing fancy without much substance, but as time passed, we witnessed some of the rapport that existed between Jing and that hawk. The two of them were like something out of a movie — somewhere between remarkable and spooky. More by accident than design, they too ended up becoming part of the Hole in the Coral Wall Gang.

However, given the current situation in which Will and I found ourselves — this Coiba Island thing — it didn't seem logical to bring a whole convoy of people to the island. We just didn't need to draw that kind of attention. If that place was remotely similar to the way Diego described it, we needed to be subtle — to slip in with my plane, quietly work our way into the jungle, snatch up the bottles of ancient "magic juice," and get the hell out. No marching bands, no parades, no fireworks. But a backup team strategically positioned somewhere close by, if something happened to go awry, made good sense.

So, first thing, I brought Diego with me up to my canal home on Big Pine Key. There was plenty of room to let us both decompress and no one to bother us. Key West was generally a madhouse about this time of the year.

There was, of course, my companion, Shadow, my huge German shepherd-Rottweiler mix, who took Diego a bit by surprise. (Shadow had been staying with my beautiful neighbor, but he came flying over the fence that was supposed to contain him when he heard my voice.) Seeing such a huge dog charging at us, Diego was already bolting for the mangroves but I caught him, grabbed Shadow (who almost knocked me over in his enthusiasm), and introduced everybody. *Lord, it was good to see my boy again...*

During the next few days, we began laying out a plan. Diego was definitely spooked by the idea of going back to Coiba, but he had little to no magic juice left in his vial. He had rolled the dice and used the majority of it to convince us so there was no choice, really. And he knew he would probably never stumble on a better opportunity to get in and out of that cursed island than with me and my friends and our...*resources.*

After a couple of days of R&R, I called Will and had him come up. According to Diego, the island was roughly thirty miles off the west coast of Panama — about twenty miles long north to south, and ten miles wide east to west.

Diego recalled that there was a small lagoon on the southwestern side. He was certain we could get my 182 in there. The trick was getting in and out quietly because, as Diego put it, if one of the thirty mad "tribes" of prisoners discovered us, we would be complaining to Jesus in person before the day was out.

I explained that I would get up high, then use a "dead-stick" approach — no power, just a wind-milling prop — basically, a glide in. Scary, but no noise at all. When we were finished with the gig, on the way out, we'd power up. At that point, it wouldn't matter if the devil himself heard us. We were getting out of town. Or, we'd simply come in on the water, using the floats like a boat, maybe just staying a couple of feet off the sea.

The truth was, the prison authorities who controlled Coiba weren't too worried about people coming in from the mainland and trying to extradite friends and relatives because, once a prisoner landed at that tropical bastion, they became incognito — impossible to find. There was never any information offered by the authorities as to where they were exactly. Maybe in the prison, maybe in the jungle, and those who ended up living in the jungle tribes were completely lost to the world, over twenty miles out to sea and buried in an angry tropical wilderness.

My friend estimated that the cave with the magic juice was about four miles inland from the lagoon. If we traveled due east we would hit a small river that bisected the lower half of the island. All we had to do was follow that south and it would take us to the last hidden walls of "the ancients' city" and the all but invisible cave with the magic juice.

It seemed easy enough, except for the government patrol boats, and the indigenous maniacs and their tribes...and the monkeys. Yeah, the howler monkeys that Diego neglected to tell us about until we were just about ready to go. You see, apparently, it maybe wasn't just the flora on this island that had taken a hit from this magic juice. One night, out on my porch, Diego reluctantly explained that a few of the creatures on the island — in particular the howler monkeys — seemed to be a bit more...*aggressive* than most.

"Great," muttered Will angrily. "Large barking monkeys. Is there anything else we need to know about — like maybe condors or small dinosaurs?"

Diego explained that there weren't many big cats on the island, maybe a couple of pairs, but the howlers were another matter. He said the sons of bitches were everywhere, and they were about a third larger than their counterparts on other parts of the globe. They were nearly forty pounds and often over four feet tall. Aside from being large and aggressive, they were loud as hell. Their incessant hooting howls — almost a barking — could make a person crazy.

At this point, we were already "in for a penny, in for a pound" as my old English mother would say. Besides, we weren't buying property. We were just visiting.

"So," I said, "we come in on a dead-stick landing, park my girl in the little pond, and head inland as fast as our little feet will carry us, huh?"

Diego nodded.

Will, ever the cautious adventurer, shook his head. "I don't like this much, with the big cats and the crazy sons of bitches in the prisoner jungle tribes."

"Then there's the cave with the magic juice," I said with a grin, trying to lighten things a little. "And the barking monkeys. I'm looking forward to that."

■ ■ ■

The following day, we met with Travis and Cody (who we had spoken with briefly on the phone), and the kids — Tax and Jing — at Crazy Eddie's Bar and Swill. It was a table of T-shirts, Cargo shorts, and blue jeans. There were no stylish dressers in our group, just island folks. There were a few things to be worked out, questions to be asked, and decisions to be made.

First off, this was not a happy-go-lucky treasure adventure. Will and I and our new friend were going into a place that there was no easy way out of if the prop quit turning, and there was absolutely no point in making this a family expedition. But a standby team made good sense and Tax and Jing simply could not be talked down. They didn't like the sound of this — a horrible prison, free-roaming maniacal prisoners in tropical gangs, snakes, spiders, giant monkeys with bad dispositions, big cats. (Okay, not many cats, but how many does it take to kill you?) And getting a plane in and out being tricky at best... But our people were going to be waiting for us offshore, on close-by islands or the coast of Panama. At the very least, as a reserve.

Then, on an additional plus side, there was the magic juice... Granted, with our most recent expeditions — the discovery of pirate treasure in the Caribbean and an Egyptian hoard of wealth in the Southwest — none of us needed money. But being part of something that could change the world — that was a big draw. To perhaps be remembered as the people who changed the planet...maybe *saved* the planet... Now, that would be cool.

I remember how Will put it in his defining, lecture-like diatribe at Crazy Eddie's. He glanced around at everyone sitting at the table.

"This planet is in serious trouble," he said. "We're losing landmasses around the globe, literally by the day. The seas are rising, the poles are melting, and there are more great storms, hurricanes, tsunamis, inland droughts, and floods than ever before. Still, even with this knowledge, we are tearing out our oxygen-making forests and jungles with the fervor of mad children. We're killing our rivers, poisoning our seas, and gradually sucking Mother Nature dry. The poor old lady is trying, but we're destroying her day by day, unceremoniously burying her in industrial waste, gas fumes, plastics, and pesticides."

Will continued, unable to stop. "In the greatest of ironies, nearly everything we tout as making our lives easier and better is actually gradually destroying this once incredible, near-perfect golden goose." My friend drew a breath. "What we are talking about here — this ability to enhance and preserve Mother Nature— might literally be a gift from heaven." There was a pause and he exhaled. "But sometimes what we wish for is the last thing we really need," he muttered cautiously. "It might be the coup de grâce for the planet." He looked around. "From the heart of Africa to the heart of America, less than a quarter of the population of this planet actually practices birth control." He took a breath and exhaled. "Almost all of Africa, a good portion of Asia, much of Central America, and certainly most of the once pristine Caribbean Islands now consist of people whose primary entertainment is mindlessly making babies."

I couldn't help myself. I had to say the words. "My friend is right. These folks have the planet preservation mentality of children. They have literally screwed themselves into poverty, and now they're destroying the environment by catching, killing, and eating anything that moves or swims around them, regardless of the dire, long-term implications to nature. If they can't eat it, they sell the skin or the horns, or the fins or the teeth…"

"And the whole process is continually exacerbated by well-meaning people in beautiful homes thousands of miles away," Will added bitterly, "who are coaxed into 'helping the starving children' by continually donating money — of which only the smallest portion ever makes its way to the desired destination."

I looked at my friends. "You see, the truth is, the more 'helpless' people you feed, the more helpless people you make. And as coldly honest as it sounds, the brightest people aren't generally the ones making babies they can't take care of. They know better. What we're producing worldwide, what we would be left with if there was food enough for all, is a collage of totally dependent, borderline cretins." I sighed. "We don't just need better vegetables. What we need is a more conscientious people eating them."

Diego nodded and smiled, his green eyes lighting in agreement. "First you fix de leak, amigo, then you mop de floor. Not the other way around."

"Spoken like a true optimist," replied Will.

It was Travis, who sat quietly in the back of the booth with his adventurous buddy, Cody Joe, who summed it up. "Diego's right. First, we get — or *you* get — the magic juice. I don't see much worth in trying to talk you out of this, so what we need to form is a support group on mainland Panama, and offshore of this island, with the equipment and communications just to monitor you if all goes well. Or…if things don't go so well, to perform an extraction." He paused and looked around the table.

There was no disagreement. There rarely was when Travis spoke.

"We'll probably need Eddie's Grumman Goose here so we have land and water access," continued Travis, looking at Eddie.

Our old adventurous friend just grinned. "Just give me a heading, dudes. Eddie's good to go."

I glanced over at Tax and Jing. Being new members of this prestigious gang, they had been relatively quiet during the conversation.

"You good to go, too?"

Tax just nodded. His eyes said it all. For an adventurous guy like him, it didn't get much better than this.

Jing pretty much summed it up. "It's not every day you have a chance to change the world," she said with a smile.

■ ■ ■

While we began preparations for our next foray into adventure, Will once again contacted his "cougar" lady friend at Miami's main library branch. He discovered that Julie had an electronic connection with the libraries in Barcelona and Madrid, which she made available to Will. The price was an evening with his lady friend. Well, a night really, and a morning and part of that afternoon…before he could pull himself away, limp and disheveled (more limp in some places than others) but very pleased all the way around.

In the process, Will discovered a fairly interesting

dissertation by one of the Spanish captains who led the conquistadors against the Cacique Indians on Coiba Island. Beyond his obvious pride in the conquest, there were some interesting if not odd statements. Captain Manuel Garcia spoke of incredible plants and fruits — huge, hillside gardens the likes of which they had never seen, and that grew almost overnight. But the Spanish had no real interest in agriculture. They were focused mostly on conquering/destroying whoever was in their path, and taking what precious metals and gems the vanquished possessed. Leaving them socially decimated and rife with European diseases wasn't actually part of the plan, but it didn't bother them in the least.

But in their myopic greed, they often destroyed knowledge that would have changed the world. The innocuous little island of Coiba was only a comma in the monstrous New World conquest by Spain, and in their haste, it appeared they overlooked an ancient prize. It didn't shine, and it wouldn't buy rank and position, but it was a remarkable trophy. And it remained hidden…

Interestingly enough, while most of the writings of the Indians and others had been destroyed, there were a few clay documents that had survived and ended up in Barcelona. They had been translated as well as possible, given the difficulty between the two languages, and there were some significantly intriguing paragraphs in the writings about plants and potions, star people, and the Blood of the Gods. It seemed the indigenous peoples possessed at least a peripheral connection to something or someone out of the ordinary. Something that "touched the hearts of growing things…and gave them spirit…"

But the truth was, if it wasn't shiny and valuable, the monarchs and ecclesiastics of Spain didn't really give a shit about it. Once they had either exterminated or converted the local residents (whichever was the easiest), they were on their way, looking for more heathens and gold.

Once again, the phrase slipped inside my friend's head…

Terraformation — the hypothetical process of deliberately modifying the atmosphere, topography, and/or ecology of a planet to make it more habitable for Earth-like life.

Giving them spirit…

Terraformation….

CHAPTER SIX

While we purchased supplies, checked our weapons, and loaded equipment into Eddie's Goose, I had the bullet holes in my amphibian repaired and everything, from electronics to mechanics, checked twice. Coiba Island ranked near the top few places in the world where you wouldn't want a mechanical or electronic failure — no AAA trip service, no convenience stores, no motels, and not a single phone booth anywhere. There was a place to stay, assuredly, but you had to have a reservation booked through Panama's Department of Corrections.

Diego informed us that the folks at the prison did have a lightweight radar system but it was poorly monitored, which meant we had to be "low and sneaky," as Will put it.

The plan was for both planes (the Goose and my 182) to fly into different small municipal airports near Santa Catalina by the coast, about forty miles northeast of Coiba Island. Then, over a twenty-four-hour period, we would move the two seaplanes to a small dot of a nothing island called Jicaron, about ten miles southwest of Coiba.

Jicaron Island was billed as the ultimate catch-and-release sportfishing experience nearly fifty miles off Panama's west coast, apparently for people who were looking for the seriously "primitive sportfishing challenge." It was, however, a perfect staging base for us. From lift-off in Jicaron to landing in Coiba, (staying close enough to the surface to practically bounce the floats) would be less than ten minutes. There was almost no way for the simple radar at the prison to pick us up or the personnel to act on anything. And we would have Eddie and his Goose on Jicaron, with Travis and Cody, ready as a backup.

There was one serious point of contention, however, that Will and I ultimately lost on. Tax and Jing insisted on going in with us — flying into the island. There was some serious fur and feathers in the air for a while regarding that. My friend and I were, of course, dead against it. But in the end, it was Travis who helped make the decision. He said that at the very least, they could watch the plane — it would be a seriously screwed-up situation if we managed to get the magic juice only to find that the howler monkeys or a couple locals on the island had found the plane and disabled it in some fashion.

As much as I hated the idea, it was a reasonable argument. Actually, we were won over by the fact that Jing had her hawk with her, and that creature had the senses of a fox as well as being silently deadly. (I would have loved to have brought Shadow but we were stretching the complications as it was.) At least I felt better knowing Travis and Cody would be standing by on Jicaron Island.

Maybe this was going to be okay… We were indeed hoping that all the crazy shit was behind us.

Ahh, but then, only gamblers and fools believe in storybook endings. As it turned out, there was one soul already intent on putting an end to our story well before it was underway…

■ ■ ■

Señor Mateo Preces, the Panamanian judge who had lost a son and replaced him with blind wrath, was still BB-spitting crazed that we (well, Diego in particular) had escaped him at the airport. He was really big on everyone getting what they deserved, as Diego could attest. He'd had one of his people pull the flight records at the airport FBO, and less than two hours after we were in the air, he was already laying plans to find Diego in this place called "Key West." By morning of the following day, he had two gunmen packing up. They would fly out of Santiago the next day.

■ ■ ■

After less than forty-eight hours of preparation, we were pretty much ready to go. The gear was packed, weapons, ammo, and portable radios were artfully hidden in my Cessna 182 floater and Eddie's Goose, and both planes were fueled. I knew what we were doing was dangerous as hell, but the smell of gun oil, gasoline, and adventure filled my nostrils and left me damned near trembling with anticipation. We were on the road again...gamblers and fools that we were.

It all might have gone just as we planned but the gods, they require a sacrifice sometimes, and you never know when they'll take it…

■ ■ ■

The evening before we were going to depart on this new adventure, we all got together at Eddie's Bar and Swill for a celebratory lift-off. It was a beautiful, crisp, Key West winter night and we were seated around "our table" toward the front, near the windows, but against a side wall for that simple degree of security that you come to grow accustomed to if you often take stupid chances.

Travis had just excused himself to use the restroom, Will was telling another of his stories, and the drinks had settled in just enough to ignite that warm feeling of invulnerability in us all, when two men came in. They were fairly large fellows with a Latin look about them — dark hair swept back, black pants, white shirts, windbreakers, and shiny shoes that said they weren't tourists. Half of our group had their backs to them. I was thinking that the two didn't really look like tourists as they paused and glanced around. When they saw us, they traded a look that I didn't like and their eyes changed. I was just raising my hand to interrupt Will when both men reached inside their light jackets. It was about that time that everything slowed down, becoming distinctly and unpleasantly memorable.

I could see Travis coming out of the restroom easily twenty feet behind the two men as they were pulling pistols from their coats. My eyes went wide and I brought up a hand but Cody, at the edge of our table, with the reflexes of a cat, was already rising and starting to yell a warning. But he had no weapon.

I'll never forget what I saw then. Cody was out of his seat in a second. He grabbed both Tax and Jing next to him by the backs of their shirts and jerked them onto the floor, then turned to the two men, yelling at them, deliberately drawing their attention. They took it and they shot him. The explosion of the weapons in the room shocked everyone. Will and I were frozen to our seats, helplessly watching Cody stagger backward and collapse, all of us barely able to draw a breath.

Tax, ever the protector of his sister, reached over and dragged her under the table. He was foolishly coming back up when Travis, still a good five or ten yards behind the two Latins, snatched up a chair from a table next to him, hefted it with one heavily muscled arm, and threw it.

Now, you have to understand the average healthy person couldn't throw one of those bar chairs five feet. But Travis was a huge guy — six foot six and seriously adrenalized. The chair soared across the short distance like a meteor, striking both men, knocking the gun from one and bowling them over for a moment. Before they could draw a breath, our huge friend was on them like a leopard. I could literally hear him snarling. The man scared me a little normally, but that night was something I'll never forget.

As one of the assailants tried to rise with his pistol, Travis stepped in, grabbed the man's hand, then twisted and snapped downward. You could hear the arm dislocate from the shoulder with a sickly pop. The man screamed and dropped his gun.

Travis was growling now — I swear to God...there was a growl coming from deep within his chest and his hard green eyes were on fire. I was terrified — and he was on my side! He jerked the fellow's arm upward, just for the pleasure of it. As the guy screamed again, Travis grabbed him by the throat. He twisted brutally, crushing the guy's windpipe. In just seconds, the assassin's eyes went from shock to indifference. The second man — the guy hit by the chair — was struggling to stand and was bringing up his weapon. But Tax was on him from behind, leaping across the room and hammering the fellow between the shoulder blades with a flying sidekick. Travis stepped in again, eyes still on fire, reaching down and grabbing that guy by the throat with one hand, lifting him into the air as if he were a rag doll. He was staring him in the face and squeezing the life from him without conscience. It took Will, me, and Tax to break the grip that would have killed the man. *We needed someone alive to find out what had brought on this attack.*

In the background, I could hear a distant siren. Eddie was in front of the bar now with his trusty twelve-gauge shotgun, monitoring the crowd, most of which were freaked out and cowering.

"Hold him," our huge friend growled to me, nodding to the gunman who was still alive, and in a second he was at Cody's side.

Cody Joe had taken a round in the upper chest, below his collarbone. It was a damned serious situation, especially if a lung or an artery was punctured. Travis knelt and lifted his friend, cradling him in those big arms, and pressing his hand against the wound, trying to slow the blood flow. "Always the showoff," he whispered, brushing the hair back from Cody's face with the gentleness of a mother. "Just relax now, amigo, no more jumping or yelling or showing off, okay?"

Through the blood and the pain, Cody Joe smiled. "Okay…" he rasped. "If you think you can handle it."

The medics arrived three minutes in front of the police. In just seconds they were compressing Cody's wound, starting IVs, and getting him on a stretcher. Travis didn't want to leave his friend but in moments the authorities would be there and any chance for information would disappear in legalities. He knelt and looked at Cody as we all stood around, helpless. "I have something I have to take care of, amigo," he whispered, his hand going to his friend's good shoulder. "Before the police arrive…"

In a flash, he was up and across the room, near the back by the restrooms where Tax and I were holding the other gunman. We had bound his hands with his own belt. The man seemed to have recovered from his throttling, and his eyes were concerned but he wasn't cowering.

Travis squatted next to him, his eyes on fire. "I want to know who and where they are…"

The guy started to reply with something confident and glib but before the fellow had managed half the words, Travis' hand shot out and grasped his throat. The power and the shock were startling.

My friend leaned in, drawing the Buck knife he carried at his side. "I'm not the law, I don't play by their rules, and I don't have much time, so either you tell me what I want to know or I'm gonna cut you in ways you'll never be able to forget."

The guy was definitely more concerned now. You could see it in his eyes, but he was still banking on legitimacy to save him. Too bad he didn't know Travis' history.

"I no give you anything, gringo. This is America…you can't just —"

Travis jerked him up without another word and kicked open the bathroom door. He looked at Tax and me. "Just watch the door." He paused and his green eyes were terrible. "Don't come in, you hear me? No matter what." Then he dragged the Latin through the door.

As Tax and I stood outside, we could just hear Travis' heavy voice, then a defiant reply again. That was it. The next thing I heard was a shuffle and a gurgling, muffled scream. A moment passed. Then there was a second high-pitched scream — a composite of terror and pain. Now we could hear the man gushing out unintelligible words, then he cried out again — another high octave amalgam of panic and agony. Then it got quiet. Travis came out, slipping his knife into its sheath. I'd never seen his eyes so cold and hard. Behind him, on the tiled floor, I caught a glimpse of the assassin, sprawled out, his pants at his knees, the groin area of his underpants covered with blood. *(There are some places a man just can't deal with being cut up...)*

Travis looked at us again. "We get Cody taken care of now, then we saddle up at dawn."

■ ■ ■

Later that afternoon, after Cody was out of intensive care and the rest of us were laying out plans of war, Travis made a phone call. He was calling in one of the dozens, maybe hundreds of favors he had earned in a couple of different conflicts. By the following morning, when Cody was doing better — breathing on his own and mumbling banters back and forth with Travis — three men showed up. Big men. Guys with hard eyes that were only tempered by the respect and affection they had for Captain Travis Christian, helicopter pilot and soldier extraordinaire. They owed him and they were honored to pay that debt. Travis called them "babysitters"...for a few days, maybe longer.

The following morning, our two planes — Eddie's Goose and my 182 — rose out of Key West Airport and headed across the pond. There was an island we had to visit, and some revenge to deal with.

Landing and Customs in the city of Santiago went without a hitch (Eddie had all the really "important, noisy stuff" hidden in his specially designed hideaways in his Goose). We spent the night in Santiago, then hooked back down to a tiny airport at the small town of Madre Vieja, just above Santa Catalina. After booking rooms at a nondescript little motel, we laid plans for a couple of reconnaissance flights over/near Coiba Island. The little dirt strip at Madre Vieja was tight for the Goose but Eddie could handle it, and there weren't many eyes there. Our team could organize without too much concern.

But we had made a collective decision. There wasn't one of us who didn't want Señor Preces' balls tacked to the wall, but if we took him on first, we would seriously muddy the waters for our mission regarding the Blood of the Gods. The death/ disappearance of a high-ranking official would bring out authorities everywhere.

On the other hand, if we got lucky, the magic juice mission could be a quick "in and out" thing. Then, once the juice was secured, we could take our time with Señor Preces.

After some debate, we finally chose to get the juice first. Like Tax said, "When you get a chance to change the world, man, you gotta take a shot."

So, off we went, on our way down the yellow brick road in pursuit of a couple of bottles of planet-changing elixir.

I remembered a saying by Rufus. It seemed appropriate. *"Sometimes you're the sails, mon. Sometimes you're the wind... The trick is knowing what is best at the time."*

CHAPTER SEVEN

Jicaron Island was quite a pretty little nook in the middle of the Pacific Ocean — palm trees, a nice lagoon, wonderful reefs, and a primitive but acceptable little lodge built just off one of the pristine beaches on the southern end. But right now we were concentrating on pulling off a snatch-and-run under the radar of the fortress prison on Coiba and we didn't have time for out-island amenities.

Will, myself, Diego, and now the kids, were preparing to fly my 182 into the little island of Jicaron and find a quiet mooring where we could stay tucked away for an hour or two. Travis and Eddie would come into Jicaron right behind us in the Goose, strictly as a backup if things went south in Coiba for some reason.

Before dawn the next morning, Will and I (and the gang) would skip across the eight miles of water to a small cove in Coiba that Diego knew about. As previously planned, and much to their disappointment, Tax and Jing (and her remarkable hawk) were assigned to the protection of the plane. If anything happened to that, we would be royally screwed.

Will, Diego, and I would make a quick, couple-hour jaunt into the interior of the island, find the cave, grab the bottles of magic juice, and beat a path back to the plane. Then we'd be in the air and gone — just a memory, a whiff of smoke. And we'd have all this crazy prison island/magic juice shit behind us.

What could possibly go wrong in a simple couple hours' hike? Huh?

Well, for one thing, there was Archo Coco…

■ ■ ■

As it turned out, there was one other soul on the island who was also hoping all the crazy shit was behind him, although he pretty much knew it wasn't. Archo Coco, once a relatively successful horseracing jockey, sometimes common thief, and pretty much always a con man, had been on the island for just over six months, which meant he was a survivor of some sort, but not a happy one. He had recently been released from *la fortaleza del infierno* (the fortress from hell) on the other side of the island after serving time there for stealing a car from Manuel Noriega's former mistress.

How in the name of the gods of hell was he supposed to know it belonged to her? It was a nice car parked outside a nightclub, so he hot-wired it and rode off. How did he know he was going to run into a freaking train? Or that the arrogant puta would have such a fit about it? Si, the car was not so nice after that, but it really wasn't his fault. Jesus! Most of the pieces were still there. And, if the police would not have chased him with such passion, he would not have tried to squeeze through the railroad gates to begin with. He explained all this to the "cabron arrogante" of a judge. But the fellow was obviously not a man of insight or compassion. So here he was, a soul of intellect and passion, in this stinkin' jungle, hiding from slavering idiotas who would screw a monkey without conscience or concern, then eat it... And if these old compadres of his caught him, they might well treat him like a luckless monkey...

Archo was out of the prison from hell but he still had six months to serve on the island itself. He had recently tried to hook up with a couple of the clans without much success.

But mother of God! Those people were all such bare-assed freaking locos! He would rather live in the trees with the freaking howler monkeys! Si, it might be true that he was a creature who took his pleasures where he could find them, and sometimes "borrowed" things without conscience, but the creatures who had been released onto this island were beyond ruthless sonabichee bastards. They were self-made monsters!

Now he found himself struggling through the horrible jungle, hiding in the trees like a freaking monkey, all because he stole a man's shoes! Well, most of his food too, and his hat — Shit! Shit! Shit! Nobody got a sense of humor on this piece-of-shit island!

■ ■ ■

Will, Diego, and I stood on the beach in the morning sun, staring out at the sparkling green sea. Tax and Jing sat in the warm sand near us, speaking quietly. Travis and Eddie were double-checking the engines on the Goose, which was moored in the shallow water about a hundred yards away.

Diego exhaled, squinting at the sun for a moment, then he turned. "Well, amigos, no use putting things off." He sighed. "Time to go."

I looked at Will and he sighed too, then nodded. "Ya mon, I guess it's time to go. Let's put this behind us — just another bar tale that no one believes."

We did a quick recap with the backup team, and Eddie assured us that "all would be groovy, man — just a walk in the freaking park." No one said goodbye. This was just a quick little gig and we'd be back on the mainland for dinner.

Ten minutes later, I was drawing back my controls to the roar of the big Lycoming engine and sensing that "release" with the earth as we became a creature of the sky, the wind, and the sun. It was pretty exciting, even though we'd done it once or twice before.

The trip from Jicaron to Coiba was totally uneventful — and all of about ten minutes — skipping over the surface of the green-blue water like a dragonfly. I barely had the engine humming and it was already time to back off the power, touch down, and move along on the surface as Diego directed me. Quite fortunately, there was a huge outcropping of stone that stared at the sea, barely into the jungle, that Diego had used as a landmark before. He spotted it and pointed, and I obeyed like I was being paid. There was a small cove and a mangrove creek at the same spot — a tributary of the small river we would follow to the cave. I eased the plane into the thick jungle via the creek. Once out of sight from the ocean, I shut the girl down as quickly as possible — no more noise than necessary. We manually squeezed a turnabout and aimed ourselves toward the sea and Will tied us off to some mangroves. (I had learned the hard way that you should always have your "going out" plans made as you're going in.) We were pretty proud of ourselves. It looked like we had pulled off a fairly quiet entrance, and under the direction of Diego, we were on our way to the creek that would take us to the cave and the magic juice. However, we would have been less happy if we had known about the pair of squinty brown eyes watching us from the jungle with a good degree of interest.

■ ■ ■

Archo Coco squatted in the mangroves, still holding his dick (which he had been using moments before this apparition appeared), his bobble-like black eyes bright with interest. *Jesus Christe! An apparition of hope! A freaking gift from the gods! Delivered to him on a plate!*

He tucked himself away and eased down a little more, his instincts heightened. The question was, why would someone be sneaking onto this island when everyone on this freaking piece of shit wanted to sneak off? *He could probably distract the gringa and gringo they had left for a moment or two, and just go hide in a luggage compartment of the plane (assuming there was a luggage compartment) and hope for the best. But...what was a bunch of gringos doing sneaking into this island?* His curiosity, which had gotten him into trouble more than once, was piquing. He eased down a little more and waited.

■ ■ ■

Inside a couple of minutes, Will and I had organized our gear — a special container for the magic juice, machetes for the resistant jungle, water, a few protein bars, and weapons (most of us carried semiautomatic pistols and a handful of magazines). Then we checked our radios. Both Will and I had one — set to an unpopular frequency with the radio in the Cessna. We didn't really expect any serious contact with anyone at this end of the island, and if that happened, the radios and the pistols would be good things to have.

What we didn't know was that Manuel Noriega's Corrections Division had recently, and quite secretly, updated the radar at the prison on Coiba. The tower there had reported what appeared to be the approach of a bogey on the far end of the island.

The jungle was a loosely congested collage of vibrant, colorful, living things. It was incredibly beautiful — like something out of an exotic nature documentary — and you could barely walk ten feet without having to trim something with your machete. We were constantly entertained by the hoots and antics of the howler monkeys in the trees around us. In addition, there was a huge variety of colorful birds constantly calling and moving in vivid sheets across the canopy above us.

It took us the better part of an hour to get to the creek that would take us to the cave (and the magic juice). The flowers, fruits, trees, plants, birds, and even some animals were twice the size of their contemporaries on the mainland and twice as dramatic in color. Everything was stunning — huge and colorful beyond common explanation. (But then, there was an explanation, and we were here for it.) It seemed impossible that this place had been somehow ignored. Will said it just showed you what an inept government of selfish, stupid bastards could accomplish.

Finally, after forty-five minutes of following the creek, we came to a place where the terrain and flora changed slightly. If you studied it for a moment, you could see the shadows of ancient walls disguised by leaf and flower. There was a strange feeling of ancient insight and you could see places, as Diego had described, where it seemed that perhaps another more advanced hand had touched it. Not enough to change the indigenous artists, but just ever so subtly adding a brushstroke of greater intellect here and there. It was both exciting and extraordinarily odd. I thought what this must have been like to see it for the first time a thousand years ago…and I suddenly found myself hating the Spanish conquistadores. But then, we'd all been conquistadores at one time or another, hadn't we?

With cautious steps, Diego led us through the maze of leaf, vine, and the ancient handicraft of man until he came to a weathered rock wall. It was so ancient it was hard to tell where the wall stopped and the low cliffs began. He carefully moved along the wall for a few moments, pulling new and old growth away here and there — vines and bushes. Diego stopped and slowly pushed back a battery of heavy growth revealing a small, dark entrance — less than a foot or so wide and maybe only four feet high. He turned to us, his face an amalgam of hope and fear. "Here it is," he breathed. "Here…"

One by one, we pulled out our flashlights and slipped through the slit in the rock into an ancient yesterday. As our flashlights blushed the interior, Diego moved over to a far wall and began brushing it with his hands, pressing here and there. Suddenly, he whispered an exclamation and the wall next to him silently inched open about a foot. He looked at us.

It was a narrow entrance but it was an invitation we couldn't refuse. I shrugged, somewhere between excited and spooked. "Lead on, amigo…"

We eased into the next room, our flashlights casting smoky yellow beams across the floor and walls. And there he was, sitting against the wall — the skeleton Diego had first described to us, as if resting. But a close look told us he didn't die easy. As

Diego had described, there were several fractured ribs, a broken arm, and a fracture in the skull.

Will shrugged. "It's obvious this fellow had a serious accident of some sort..."

But the real prize was above the skeleton. Above the bones of the ancient soul, carved into the wall in that same flowing, polished fashion, was a shelf. On the shelf were three glass-like containers about the size of large whiskey flasks. Just as Diego had described, the glass was dark, like ancient rum bottles.

"It seems strange, this fellow being left here," Will muttered, studying the scene. "It feels almost like they were in a hurry and they left him because he was dying...or dead."

"Something happened here," I said quietly, almost to myself. "An accident or maybe a conflict of some sort with the locals...I don't know. Whatever it was, they were flustered enough to leave the magic juice. I think they thought they would come back, but they didn't."

Without any formality, Will slipped off his pack, which had a specially padded pocket for the bottles. We loaded them with the consideration of nitroglycerin, locked the pack down tightly, and my friend slipped it on again. We all stood there for a moment in the dusty gloom of the flashlights.

Will smiled and looked at me, breaking the moment. "C'mon, Tonto, let's get the hell out of here."

"How many times do I have to tell you..." I replied, holding up a finger.

Diego looked at us. "What is this Tonto thing between you two?"

We just smiled.

"You hang around long enough, maybe you'll get to be Tonto," I said with a grin. And with no more than a "Hi-ho Silver!" we were gone.

■ ■ ■

But all was not as good as it seemed. Hidden in the dense underbrush only fifty feet away, Archo Coco eased back on his haunches and cocked his head. "What you suppose dese crazy gringos are up to?" he said to himself.

Coco would have liked to have had a look in that cave, but the big prize was the gringos and their airplane. So he followed.

■ ■ ■

The sun was past its zenith but we were making pretty good time, and everything was rolling along just as we planned. I was beginning to feel fairly confident. We stopped for a moment to adjust our packs when out of the woods around us stepped four soldiers with automatic weapons.

The officer (I assumed by his shoulder insignias) stepped forward, his pistol out. He smiled. It wasn't pretty. Actually, *he* wasn't that pretty either. There was a shoddiness to the soldiers' uniforms and they all looked like they could use a shave and a haircut. I remembered a friend of mine once telling me about what he called "outpost soldiers" stationed in remote situations, and how they often lost their "decorum." These folks had definitely lost their decorum and its companion, pride.

"I would like to say chu are some pretty lost gringos," said the officer as he waved a forefinger. "But somehow, I don' think so." He shoved the pistol at us. "Drop your guns. Now," he growled. "Dere is no money on courage here. Do what I say!"

When our weapons had been collected, the officer stared at us. "What chu do here?" he asked, throwing out his hands. "Chu looking for a friend who is a guest of dis island?" He sighed and shook his head. "Chu wouldn't be de first gringos to do this stupid thing. In the end, all you do is get a new home for a while." He barked over his shoulder to his lieutenant, "Search them!"

In moments, they were going through our packs and found the bottles. Remarkably enough, they didn't get stupid and break anything right away.

One of the soldiers pulled out a bottle of our "miracle-grow" (which, I will admit, looked almost exactly like a high-end liquor flask). "*Bueno!*" he growled, pleased with himself. He looked around. When his officer didn't offer disapproval, he twisted off the cap and sniffed it.

The officer looked at us, noticing the tension immediately. "Nice of you to bring a gift for us." He took the bottle from his soldier, held it up, and shrugged. "Brandy, eh? Cognac? And aged, I would say, no? You no be da first smugglers in this place."

I glanced at Will and Diego and read their eyes. This was terrible but there wasn't much we could do. As soon as we told these idiots it wasn't liquor, but something much more valuable, we'd never see it again. Hell, there was a good chance no one would ever see *us* again. But at that moment, I noticed something…

At first, I thought it was my eyes playing tricks on me. A face appeared in the foliage behind the soldiers — grimy, disheveled, and plague thin with dark, interested eyes and dirty black hair hanging down in curly ringlets. Then it was gone. I shook my head — *an apparition or something?* But I wasn't given an opportunity to figure it out. At the same time, the soldier with the bottle of magic juice was smelling it, then lifting it to his lips for a taste. I raised a hand, then caught myself. What the hell could we do? We sure as hell couldn't tell them the truth.

The man shook his head with a shiver. "It has a bit of a bite to it, my friends," he muttered with a shrug. "But I have had worse."

"For God's sake, man, I wouldn't do that," said Will. "That's not…"

But the guy was already taking another small hit, then passing it to his second in command. "Don' worry, amigos, we leave you a little," he said to us. "It may be the last liquor you taste for a while." His friend took a swig and passed it on.

Diego was about to have a fit and looked like he was going to rush them. I grabbed his arm. But by the time the last soldier was reaching for the bottle, the officer was looking seriously uncomfortable. His eyes had the look of a man receiving particularly bad news. And indeed, the news was bad.

The officer moaned. "This is not good. No, not so good..." he whispered as he slipped to his knees and coughed, gasping.

Seconds later, the man behind him offered a guttural moan and suddenly clutched his stomach, collapsing like a rag doll. In seconds they were gasping and puking like "first drunk" teenagers.

At the same time, I noticed the mysterious disheveled creature again. He was closer now, at the very edge of the clearing. I could make out dirty cotton pants, a battered T-shirt, tattered tennis shoes, and he was holding a large stick. The third guy had stumbled to his knees, only seconds behind the others, now headed toward serious projectile vomiting.

But the problem was, the last soldier hadn't taken a taste before all the bad news arrived. He brought up his weapon and aimed it at us as he backed away from everyone. "You poison my friends," he growled.

The accusation was reinforced by his companions as they replied in a chorus of unfettered puking.

"You gottdam gringos," the man seethed as he moved back against the jungle, eyes locked on us, his gun at his shoulder now. "You don' gotta worry about dis island hurting you. I fix you!"

As he spoke, I noticed the grubby apparition again, still holding his stick, slipping up in the thick greenery right behind the guy with the gun. The last soldier offered an ugly smile, his finger on the trigger.

We all yelled (okay, it was more like screaming and begging) and stumbled backward. But before the soldier pulled the trigger, the apparition stepped up and whacked him into next Tuesday. However, our new, somewhat disheveled savior wasn't done. He stepped in and yelled at the puking officer and his kneeling companions spread out around him — some seriously foul stuff in a couple of different languages — and whacked everyone a few times, just for good measure. He apparently had some issues with these boys.

"Man, that's an angry son-a-bitch!" I whispered, somewhere between grateful and fearful.

"I don't care who he is, or what he is. I wanna kiss him on the lips," Will said incredulously.

Diego was the first to react. He was up, hands out, offering promises of peace and money as our friendly apparition backed away a little and straightened.

"Sons a bitches!" the odd fellow spat as he kicked the downed officer, just because. "Dey keep Archo in a cell for months, jus' because he steal a banana..." He paused. "An' a watch..." He shrugged and held out a hand. "An' a couple wallets from da barracks." He rolled his shoulders again. "But I get out. *Si*, it may be a terrible, terrible damn prison..." Then he grinned. "But de locks, de locks be made by *idiota* monkeys."

Our new friend, obviously some sort of specialist at light thievery, threw up his hands.

"Jesus on tiny crutches! Why would anybody make such shitty locks, den stamp their name on all of them — 'Made in China'...Made in China... *Jesus Christe!* It's like a warning!" He calmed down for a moment, then held up a finger. "All dis make me remember something my old, very wise *abuela* once tell me, that would be good for you *Americanos* to remember. 'Never buy soup from your enemy...'"

I couldn't help but chuckle. This guy was right on and a handful to boot. The fellow looked at the broken stick he was still holding, then down at the soldier at his feet. The fellow was groaning and struggling to sit up. The little guy hit him again, just for the hell of it. "Chu shoulda drank da medicine," he growled. Then he looked up at us. "You got gum? I no have gum in a year."

I glanced at Will.

"No gum," he said. "Sorry…"

The fellow shrugged again. "Okay…" He stared at us. "You got a way off dis island."

It wasn't a question. He obviously knew we did.

"I'n goin' with you."

It seemed like a fair trade — our lives, which he had saved, for his freedom.

"What's your name?" I asked.

The guy paused for a moment, as if he had to think about it. "Archo," he said. "My name is Archo Coco." He cocked his head. "You sure you don't got gum? How 'bout a candy bar? I really miss candy bars…"

We managed to save about half of the magic juice that was in the opened bottle. I corked it carefully, wrapped it, and put it back into the special container in the pack. Our new companion watched but didn't say anything. I think it was below his level of interest at the time. It looked like things were maybe working out, but as ol' Rufus was prone to say, *"Never count your parrots before dey in the sack."* Or something like that. Rufus was also inclined to say, *"De gods, dey love complicated entertainment."*

A half-hour later, we were back at the plane, making quick introductions with Tax and Jing. Archo didn't care much about Tax one way or the other, but Jing really struck his chimes. He'd been too long in the jungle for one thing, and she had gum. But after being introduced to her hawk, he backed off a notch.

The trek back had been uneventful, thank God, and the journey was just as breathtaking as on the way in. The trees, plants, fruits, and flowers were remarkable in their colors and extraordinary sizes. The animals and birds ran the flora a close second.

"I still think they were experimenting," Will observed under his breath, lost to the incredible experience as we stood by the plane.

"It makes me wonder how many other places might have been used as sort of a testing grounds," I added as we loaded our gear.

"Madagascar would be on the list, amigo," muttered our friend Diego.

"And Borneo and Tasmania," said Will. "From the lizards and the birds to the strange primates, as well as the plants." He shrugged. "Maybe just extraordinary experiments on occasion..."

"Yeah, yeah, yeah," growled Archo. "That all seem real nice from da outside, but you don' mention da damn-shit slithering snakes, da bitin' spiders, da freakin' screaming monkeys yellin' all da time," he paused. "And da damn big cats…" He eased out a breath and pointed at the plane. "Make da propeller move…I wanna get more gum."

CHAPTER EIGHT

The patrol boat, dispatched at the fortress commandant's orders, arrived five minutes too late. We were gone. We never left the surface on the way back to Jicaron Island, fishing capital of nowhere. Our floats just skimmed the waves and we didn't break radio silence. We were certain that, except for the hazy memories of a few soldiers (who weren't likely to report their failure), it was like we were never on Coiba.

After picking up Travis, Eddie, and the Goose on Jicaron, we flew in tandem across the blue-green waters of the Pacific, back to the little airstrip in Panama. On the flight back, we celebrated the collection of Diego's magic juice (well, most of it) and began to consider plans for the future. We were going to change the world. And get rich. Richer…

But we had something to take care of first. Travis was still on the warpath and he reminded us all that we had a friend — one of us — who lay in a hospital bed on the other side of the Caribbean, holding onto life. I recalled an old American Indian quote then, regarding revenge. "*The blade forgets, but the flesh remembers*." We hadn't forgotten about our buddy, Cody. No, we hadn't. *The flesh remembers*…

It's not an easy thing, knowing that you're going after a man to take his life. But Diego knew this man. He had dealt with him close up. He had seen the violence and the hate that the judge was known for, regardless of the situation with the death of Preces' son. The judge would bulldog this until he had removed whoever he had to just to even the score. But we were at a huge disadvantage. None of us wanted to find ourselves wanted for murder in Panama. This whole thing had to be handled with some finesse.

Oddly enough, that's where our new friend, Archo Coco, came in.

After landing and tying off our aircraft, we returned to the motel in our rental car. We got a room for Archo, and I gave him some clothes — a shirt, some jeans, and a pair of tennis shoes, all of which fit remarkably well. After a shower and a shave, and a couple of packs of gum, he looked and felt almost human.

That evening, as we sat in a nearly empty little restaurant, we began discussing our plans. Like Travis said: "It doesn't matter who you are, sooner or later everyone sits down to a banquet of consequences."

Judge Mateo Preces' banquet was coming up.

As we sat there, going over how all this came about — the killing of the judge's son and Judge Preces' revenge — we, of course, included Archo. He had just escaped prison and we would probably be turning him loose tomorrow anyway.

"Maybe you don' need to kill him, maybe you jus' need to kill his head," our new friend suddenly said, speaking of the judge.

Will turned to him. "What do you mean, 'kill his head'?"

"Mi abuela — my grandmother — she is a *bruja."* Archo paused. "Chu know, a witch." He held up a finger and wiggled it. "But she is not jus' a witch. She a got-dam scary, burn your hair off and make your eyeballs fall out witch. She is like da *primo bruja* — other witches come to her for potions." He looked around at us. "I understand da seriousness of dis thing you are in. I hear you talk about your hurt friend and dis crazy-mad judge...and Diego…" Archo looked around at us. "So I tell you, me *abuela* is da witch of witches. Her 'familiar' is a fer-de-lance — the most deadly snake in Central America. She wear it around her throat like a necklace. She talk to it. She kiss it."

"That sounds a little far out," said Will. "Where are we going with this?"

"She also got potions…potions like make you sleep, make

you crazy, make you dead…you name it," our new friend continued.

I looked over at Travis. Even though Travis Christian was more of a "meat and potatoes" kind of guy when it came to things that stepped outside common understanding, he'd been around Will and me long enough to come to appreciate the periphery of the "really crazy shit" that seemed to exist in the eaves of reality. We had caught his attention. He gave Archo a Travis Christian stare — the kind that could bubble fresh paint.

"You telling me that your *abuela* could give us a potion that could mess up his head permanently?" He paused. "I'd prefer to turn him into a frog, then step on him, but I'd settle for him *thinking* he's a frog…like, forever…"

Archo took a moment to answer, then nodded. "*Si, mi amigo,* I be pretty damn sure." He got serious. "One time I see her talk with a man for a moment — she give him something to drink too. That evening he walk out in front of a bus with a smile on his face."

"Still sounds like serious bullshit to me," muttered Travis, staring at Archo for a moment, then looking at the rest of us. "But wouldn't that be the damnedest thing…"

There were, of course, a few things that needed to happen on this walk down the yellow brick road. To begin with, we needed to find Judge Mateo Preces, then we needed him to drink a special potion cocktail. And of course, we had to get the cocktail from a crazy-assed killer witch…

I wished there was some way to glean a little more insight here before we stepped into this whole affair. I couldn't help being reminded of another crazy-assed soul we knew — Rufus — who often said, *"Insight, mon, is what you get when you survive your own stupidity."*

In the end, we decided to roll the dice. First off, Archo contacted his spooky grandmother and was granted a meeting. It was a little "potions and herbs" shop on a side road about ten miles outside Santiago at the edge of a village that could have easily been called "Nowhere" in one of Rod Serling's shows.

Will and I went in with Archo. We both spoke Spanish well and could follow what was happening, and report back to Travis and the gang.

We went inside and looked around. Surprisingly enough, there were no cobwebs and very little weird pagan or ritualistic paraphernalia in sight. There were teapots and plates here and there, one wall contained old books, and there were incense candles burning in a few places. But all in all, it was nowhere near as spooky as I had expected.

Then there was the proprietor, Archo's grandmother. And that was the real surprise.

I had braced myself for a decrepit creature with a pointed hat and a bent nose…but man, was I wrong. Sheeca was like a silky cat. Yes, she was older, but with long dark hair and a very acceptable figure, she was not at all out of the game. On the contrary, the woman purred and almost rubbed against you when she spoke, or her hand would stroke you and it felt…electric. And nice. It was a little freaky but I can't exactly say it was unpleasant.

I think if we had stayed there more than the time allotted, and not had Archo to save us and eventually push us out the door, we would have ended up in some kind of spooky ménage a trois and at best, probably awoken to find ourselves on some dirt road to nowhere with drool running down our chins, glazed eyes, and no memory of anything. I'm telling you, the woman scared and excited you at the same time. But ultimately, she leaned a little on the scary side. Mainly because, I think, through it all, you could sense a lack of conscience. There was no real understanding of compassion in those green eyes.

Anyway, I don't remember as much as I should about that whole smoky affair. But I recall that we — Archo, Will, and I — managed to explain what we wanted. There was a man who needed "fixing" — a politician. The woman's eyes lit up when we said it was a politician. Strange thing there — disease, death, and politicians — we all prefer they visit someone else. Our new acquaintance was very cooperative. It appeared that Judge Mateo Preces had chosen to imprison a fellow "practitioner of the shadow arts" a few months back — something about a friend of the judge misusing a potion and losing his eyesight for a while… So, apparently, Sheeca welcomed the opportunity to return a payment to the judge.

She offered a bitter smile and hissed quietly, "I think we will clip his wings."

I didn't know what that meant, exactly, but the glacial look in her eyes freaked me right out.

Sheeca excused herself for a few moments and went into a curtained back room. When she reappeared, she had a small vial of yellow liquid for us. "In food, in a drink, or even just a splash on the skin." Her eyes darkened. "That is all it takes, so be careful, *mis amigos*..." She shrugged. "Who knows? I might play this game with you..."

■ ■ ■

Later that day, after a brief powwow with the team, Archo, posing as a news reporter, visited the courthouse to find out what the schedule was for District Judge Mateo Preces in the next couple of days. He got to Mateo's secretary, a talkative little bird. One of the things that caught our attention was Preces' interest in a particular area of cliffs by the sea just outside of a town called Puerto Vidal. The judge was having a house built there. Apparently, he was headed out there this afternoon to have a look at the progress and was not to be bothered today.

A cliff. Hmm… By the sea. Hmmmm…

A half-hour later, we were all at the development in Puerto Vidal. The gated community wasn't gated yet, and it was mostly a few big houses in the process of construction. There were workers here and there, trucks of lumber being delivered, and a lunch wagon (Tonita's Taco Delight) that seemed to be doing a good business. Sure enough, there was the judge's big Lincoln nearby. But Preces was no fool and this was Central America, where officials sometimes lost their positions in messy fashions rather than via a ballot box. With him was a big fellow with short hair and dark sunglasses, and a bulge in the breast pocket of his light jacket. The judge was dressed casually — short-sleeved shirt and light trousers, and a wide-brimmed Panama-style hat.

There were only a few people around the lunch wagon. Not really a line but sort of a group milling about waiting to place or receive their orders — a few construction workers, a couple of folks who appeared they might be potential owners of new houses, two or three tourists, and a lady, perhaps a nanny, with a large-brimmed hat that shielded her face, keeping the hot sun at bay. She pushed a stroller where it appeared a young child rested, although the stroller roof and gauze screen pretty much obscured the child. She checked the youngster dutifully and cooed attentively.

We spread out a little so we didn't look conspicuous. I had Tax and Jing stay with our vehicle. Will and I got in line at the wagon, while the others found things to look at here and there. Diego stayed back a ways, also near our vehicle.

We needed to get close to Preces. Then I would take a shot with the magic juice. Splash the guy or get a few drops in his food. It had been unofficially agreed that if that didn't work, it was Travis' show…

The judge was in front of the woman and the baby in the stroller, impatiently gathering his food. His bodyguard was off to the side, observing the perimeter. As Preces turned with his plate, I started to move in but he and the woman bumped into each other for the briefest of moments.

One of Will's specialties was diversions. He was an artist when it came to getting attention while doing something else, so I was accustomed to sleight-of-hand maneuvers. There was something about that brief exchange and I could have sworn I saw something in the woman's hand. Did she accidentally splash something on the judge's arm? On his food? And the woman whispered something to him, a brief sentence or two. Damn, she seemed sort of familiar… Then, as she was attending to the baby in the carriage, her hat slipped to the side slightly and I saw her face. *Son of a bitch! The hot witch!* She realized that I recognized her and smiled. It wasn't exactly pretty — more like conspiratorial. Then she turned away. Right now I wasn't going to do anything that would screw our chances of a clean shot at this guy, so we were forced to back off for a moment and see what happened.

Judge Preces got his burrito supremo and headed toward the cliffs overlooking the sea. His bodyguard followed.

We all glanced at each other. I offered a hand signal telling everyone to relax for the moment and we casually followed.

Near the edge of the cliffs, the judge gazed out at the glistening sea for a moment and eased out a breath. He unwrapped his burrito and took a couple of serious bites, carefully peering out at the great blue expanse, almost fearlessly studying the rocks and beach a hundred feet below. About then, I would have sworn the look on his face began to change, softening, relaxing… The judge eased forward a little more, slowly, then halted. The man's eyes had gone strange, as if he was hearing something or seeing something that the rest of us weren't. Judge Mateo Preces shook his head. He sighed and blinked a couple of times, then shuffled closer to the precipice, his eyes growing distant.

I nudged Will but I didn't have to. He and the others had caught the show. The judge's bodyguard cautiously moved up behind and to the side of him, within reach.

"He's gonna do it…" hissed Will. "The son of a bitch is gonna do it — the hot witch's freaking potion is working… He's gonna walk off the edge…"

At the last second, as he teetered at the rim, Mateo Preces seemed to regain his senses. He shook his head and straightened up, like a man coming out of a dream. He was fighting it. He didn't know what was going on, but he was resisting. The judge exhaled heavily, straightened up, shook his mane of black hair, and hesitantly started to back away from the brink.

"Son of a bitch!" growled Travis under his breath, reaching for the pistol under his shirt.

At that moment, the bodyguard suddenly glanced around, and not seeing anyone watching, stepped in and casually shoved his boss in the back. It was the damnedest thing I'd ever seen. No emotion there — no fear, no concern. Nothing. Just a shove.

The judge's hands flew up, waving helplessly, and his eyes went wide as he teetered on the clifftop edge. He turned then, and for just a moment I'm sure he saw Diego, who had moved up next to us. Our friend couldn't help himself. He had to see this. He *had* to. Diego straightened, staring at the judge, and brought up one hand slightly, offering a short back and forth wave, his eyes filled with victory and survival.

Judge Mateo Preces gasped, then one foot slipped off the rim, his body turned, and the man's eyes suddenly filled with as much ugly surprise as any one person deserves. He twisted then and fell, with a very girlish shriek, his arms waving uselessly as gravity and the dice of life failed him.

"Dat flapping thing not gonna work," muttered Archo. "He way too fat to fly."

The bodyguard took a glance around. There was no one near to the incident except us, and we quickly became interested in the housing development behind us. The man stared at us for a moment, then casually turned and strolled away.

I looked at Will. "What the hell?" I whispered.

Travis, who was standing next to us, nodded with a good degree of satisfaction. "Sometimes you just get exactly what you deserve. Could be we were waiting in line to whack this dude and didn't know it."

"I wouldn't be surprised if the bodyguard was just a backup," said Will. "In case the potion didn't work."

"Doesn't matter," Travis said. "Game, set, match." Our big

friend eased out a breath and looked at us. “Let’s go home.”

We took the following day to lay some plans and get the planes in order for the flight back. We decided to hide the magic-grow bottles in one of the secret compartments in Eddie’s Goose. He had hiding places that a psychic on crack couldn’t find.

For his extraordinary help, we gave the most amazing Archo Coco five thousand dollars and bought him a little red sports car, which fit him just right. He actually cleaned up pretty well. Archo thought about coming back to the States with us, but that opened up a handful of situations that could have made life difficult for all of us. In the end, our new friend decided he felt better in a place where he knew all the rules and most of the players.

For the rest of us, the challenges were just beginning. The greatest challenge of all being, how do you hold on to a secret that will change the world — and live to tell about it?

Will turned to me, his eyes displaying that old adventurous sparkle. “So put me on a highway, and show me a sign…”

I smiled. “And take it to the limit one more time…”

CHAPTER NINE

The next day, we ran up the eastern coast of Central America in a convoy and spent the night in Cancun again. The following day, we shot across the Gulf of Mexico and were back in Key West and through Customs in time for happy hour that evening. And it was a pretty happy hour.

The next morning, we unloaded the planes and cautiously removed the magic juice from its hiding place in the Goose. Then I took the two full bottles to my bank in Key West and stored them in my large safety deposit box. We kept the partial bottle out — the one that the Coiba Prison soldiers had sipped from. I planned on taking that one home with me. But first on the list was to see our wounded buddy.

Cody was doing much better, as the nurses could attest to. He was sitting up in his bed, walking around, and all but chasing the attendants, and they had him set for release the following day. After reassuring ourselves as to our buddy's health, we headed off to our respective homes.

My home was on the Atlantic side of the island, about a mile or so from Travis', and Diego was staying with me for a few days until he could find a place to rent. The first thing I did when I got home was to use the old smuggler's trick of "innocuous storage" — always put something of serious value in a container of obvious minimum if not useless value. I looked around without satisfaction, then opened the refrigerator. There it was, innocuousness at its best: Doctor Johnson's Guaranteed Overnight Laxative. I emptied the laxative, washed the bottle well, then poured my remaining Crazy Grow (I don't know why, but that name seemed to have stuck in my head for some reason) into the bottle. I capped it tight and put it back on the door shelf of the fridge.

Diego smiled at my cleverness, but added, "Don' be getting drunk, amigo and forgetting…"

■ ■ ■

After everyone had enjoyed a good night's sleep, we held a morning meeting on the back porch of Eddie's bar before he opened. Today we were getting Cody out of the hospital and taking him over to stay with Travis for a while.

"So," said Eddie. "You say that this gig is about some amazing shit that makes Johnny Appleseed look like a Cuban lawn boy, huh?"

Diego, Will, and I nodded.

"That's about it," I said.

Travis shrugged. "Well, as much as I want to believe this whole thing, the proof is in the pudding." He looked around. "How about a test?" he said, pointing out the window at a new, fairly stringy bougainvillea stretching into the latticework on the back porch.

"Good as anything," Diego said. "You got a gallon jug somewhere?"

Tax and Jing stood to the side and watched, whispering back and forth with the enthusiasm of youth.

Eddie produced a plastic jug and I produced a small sample bottle of our magic elixir and poured a half-dozen drops into the jug, then filled it with water.

Eddie watched. "That's it, dude? A few drops? I want to see some results here, man."

I shrugged and put a few more drops into the jug. "This is overkill," I said. "But it'll make the point." I sighed. "Go pour it out on the ground, where the roots are."

Eddie obeyed, emptied the container, then tossed the jug onto the porch and returned. He looked at us. "If this works,

I'll..."

Will shook a finger at him. "Don't make any bets with your mouth that the rest of you can't keep," he said. "We'll all just meet here tomorrow morning about ten, okay?"

The following morning it was the same damned amazing story. The scrawny bougainvillea had puffed out overnight. Just like the first experiment on the rubber tree in Panama, it wasn't a "knock your head off" transformation, but it was obvious that something had happened. The vines and flowers were fuller, bigger, happier…

Eddie, our normally somewhat skeptical compadre, was definitely impressed. "That's pretty damned amazing," he whispered. "It's not balls on the floor, but you've gotten my attention."

Will held out his hands. "Hell, man, you gotta remember this has had less than twenty-four hours. What you have to get into your head is, what if you were able to feed this to a plant or plants a few times during a growing season?"

"I'm thinking you might have Frankenstein fruit," observed Eddie, echoing all our thoughts. "Monster mangoes… watermelons the size of Volkswagens…" He looked around at us and cocked his head, his one eye bright with intrigue. "You know what you got here, right?"

Will, Diego, and I nodded. "Ooohh, yeah…" we breathed in harmony.

"A planet changer," Eddie marveled, still looking at his buffed-up bougainvillea. "Freaking Crazy Grow shit."

"Crazy Grow…" I muttered. *Same thing I thought...* "Maybe the name of our new company…"

"Let's not get ahead of ourselves," said Will. "Baby steps…baby steps. The trick is to help the freaking world, and help ourselves but to stay alive through this."

"Crazy Grow," Eddie whispered with that half-grin of his.

Meanwhile, somewhere else...

There was no question that Key West was a magnet for thrill-seekers, the searchers of "strange," and the slightly off-center. And nearly any one of those groups could be entertaining in some respect. But it was when you put a few of those characteristics together that things got spooky.

Welcome to the Tabernacle of the Holy Bermuda Triangle. It was a church…of sorts…that had kind of borrowed several messages and incorporated them into a single, seriously off-center theme. Nonetheless, I suppose it was somewhat compelling for this handful of the spiritually uncertain, the easily confused, and the perpetually challenged in life.

The Tabernacle members' plan was to spend their annual sabbatical in Key West taking acid and "hooking up" telepathically with the aliens in the Bermuda Triangle. The problem was, Harry "The Seeker" Jones, who was a fairly important priest for the Tabernacle, had taken a small hit of acid and gotten fairly drunk the night before. He ended up getting lost and crashing under Crazy Eddie's back porch, only a few feet from the little bougainvillea that was about to get divinely anointed with Crazy Grow. The sun had set when we hit the plant with the juice, and given the shadows under the porch, no one noticed Harry. Unfortunately, Harry noticed us…and heard us talking about some sort of magical grow stuff and pouring it on the bougainvillea.

■ ■ ■

Harry awakened the next morning to the people on the porch talking again about the same magic-grow juice, and how they were going to handle its "potential." It was then that Harry noticed the frigging bougainvillea next to him was about twice the size that it was the night before, when he had watched someone pour something on it.

At first, he was certain these folks were space people — maybe the ones from the Bermuda Triangle. *But they didn't appear to have the third eye in the back of their heads. Of course, it could be covered up by hair...*

No matter, this was something significant. It could be a message from the gods or…it might just be an opportunity. Or it could be both. He might be able to help the gods and help himself if he played this right. He quieted his head. The people on the porch were talking again. They were saying that most of the stuff they called Crazy Grow was in the bank, but they did have some in a bottle. One fellow said he kept it at his house, in the refrigerator in a laxative container. Harry paused. As greedy a soul as he was, this might be just a little too big for him to handle by himself. Yeah…it might be better if he brought in Reverend Constance and her brother, Miles — seekers of truth, justice, and the Tabernacle Way.

Yeah, they would know what to do…

■ ■ ■

So, while we were getting Cody released from the hospital and settled in over at Travis' place on the gulf side of Big Pine Key, Harry the Seeker was meeting with Reverend Constance and Reverend Miles in Key West. Both Constance and Miles thought Harry was wrapped a little loose, but damn, the guy was so adamant about what he had seen, almost shaking while delivering his description. Lord knew they had believed in worse things, and the truth was, neither of them was really very cerebrally agile to begin with. But this… What made this so attractive was its potential as a money-maker. An *extraordinary* money-maker. If this whole thing was just remotely true, it was the chance of a lifetime. And hell, they'd been believing in and waiting for the arrival of the Bermuda Triangle gods for so long that the lines of any sort of truth and fantasy had pretty much blurred. (This, of course, could have something to do with all the recreational drugs they consumed while waiting.) They'd pretty much worn out the enthusiasm in the tithing business as well, so it just wasn't much of a step for them.

Miles looked at his sister.

Constance shrugged. "What have we got to lose, really?" she said. "This could be the goose with the golden legs."

"Eggs," mumbled Miles. "I think it's eggs…"

Constance wasn't the brightest bulb on the tree, but she was pretty. She liked quotes but she rarely got them right.

Miles turned to Harry. "Go get cleaned up. Don't take any more acid. Don't take shit — you hear? We may need you." As Harry walked away, Miles turned to his sister. "You go put on something sexy but not nipple-showing stupid, okay? We're gonna go to this bar and just hang out for a while. Watch and listen." He paused and grinned slightly. "Maybe this could be the big one — the big gift from our alien brothers and sisters…from the Triangle…" *(Neither of them was actually convinced there were alien brothers and sisters out there, but you do enough acid and tequila and your mind eventually gives up, and it tells you what you want to hear.)*

Constance stared at him somewhere between skeptical and hopeful.

Miles shrugged. "If any of this is real with these guys, maybe we can snatch this magic juice, sell it to the highest bidder, and ride off into the sunset."

"What about the others — the congregation?" asked his sister.

"They can get their own juice," said her brother with a smile.

■ ■ ■

It took most of the morning to get Cody settled in at Travis' place. Cody was recovering well. It appeared there would be no lingering effects from the wound. He just needed time to heal.

After an hour of getting him comfortable, we all gathered together in the living room for a conference. Will came up from Key West with Eddie, and Tax and Jing had driven up from their homes on Summerland Key. For the next hour we sat around, tossing out ideas on how to deal with the magic juice. The spectrum ran from offering it for sale to a high-level chemical company, to hiring an engineer or two and seeing if we could reproduce it. The bottom line was we only had two bottles of this stuff, and for this idea to work on a national or even worldwide level, we would need hundreds, maybe thousands of gallons. Then the question was, do we look at this as a commercially viable endeavor and become zillionaires, or do we become benefactors to the world and give the formula away…to everyone?

After some thought (and not all of the thought was greedy) we realized that someone had to control this, and it was better if that was us rather than someone we didn't know and couldn't trust. But there was no way around having this analyzed by a chemical company, because the bottom line was we had a very finite amount of Crazy Grow and we, and the world, would need lots.

We didn't really have to tell anyone what the juice did. (And no one would ever guess.) So, Will went to the phonebook and after a couple of calls, found a group in Miami called Organic Analysis Incorporated. It sounded like the right kind of place. He made a call and explained our situation — that we had a chemical substance we needed to have analyzed — and arranged for an appointment about three days out. The downside of this whole thing was, they generally required four ounces of anything to get an accurate analysis. And they needed at least two weeks for the process. Will and I both blanched. That was a lot of magic juice to give away…and a long time. But we needed to know.

■ ■ ■

The "reverends" Miles and Constance had been sitting near the back of Eddie's Bar and Swill for quite some time, and they were about to give up when Will, Eddie, and I came through the doors after our visit with Travis. We decided to move toward the back, where there was only one couple — a guy and a girl — hunched over their drinks. The girl wasn't bad looking — nice figure, medium height, dark hair to her shoulders, nice greenish eyes (but they looked like they needed to be plugged in), and a little makeup, but not "painted." The guy was maybe five eight, had a thin build, and the same hair color as the girl's, whose was long but not hippie long. He had a wiry look to him and the same green eyes, but with more animation. For some reason, he reminded me of a carnival barker — like he was looking for the next customer for the big tent.

Nonetheless, there was less traffic in the room than I expected, so we could talk and the piped-in music was probably distracting enough to allow for some privacy.

What we couldn't have known was that Miles had the extraordinary hearing of a Basenji hound. The man could make out the movement of rats in the walls of the house next door.

Sometimes the gods smile on you, and sometimes they don't.

While they weren't really able to get every detail of what we said, Miles' hearing was certainly agile enough to ascertain that we were the dudes with the magic juice, and I was the guy who put Crazy Grow in the laxative bottle in the refrigerator of my home (just as their constituent, Harry, had explained). Most importantly, they learned in a casual statement from the shorter guy that there were two more bottles in his safety deposit box.

It was extraordinary timing and luck — for them...

"I think we can do this," Miles whispered, offering something close to a smile. "I mean, it's all right here in front of us."

Constance nodded in agreement. "A turd in the hand is worth two in the bush."

Miles shook his head. *"Bird..."* he replied. *"Bird..."*

Miles and Constance were faith-based scoundrels but not necessarily bandits. They didn't like the idea of an actual confrontation if they could avoid it, and they were just smart enough to be dangerous. But this didn't seem like too tough of a situation. They had heard us mention that we would be in Key West for "Sunset," the daily ritual at Mallory Square — the closest thing to a circus coming to town, and always entertaining once you had three or four rums in you and a hit off a spliff. There was no reason why they couldn't just sneak into the guy's house and raid the refrigerator. How hard could that be? But they needed to know where the guy lived. Constance, in her low-cut floral blouse and miniskirt, stepped up for that. She wasn't anywhere near brilliant, but she had learned to use the tools at her disposal with a good degree of success.

After the two fellows had left for Sunset, and while Constance and her brother were paying their bill, she feigned forgetfulness (which wasn't too much of an act), mentioning that they were friends with the last customers and they were supposed to meet them for dinner at their house, but they forgot the address. Constance confused the guy at the register by leaning in and bending over, offering a casual "tit shot," then reaching out and touching the guy on the arm, sliding her hand down to his hand, then bending over once more to smooth the hem of her short skirt. That pretty much did it. Miles was fairly certain the guy would have given away the mayor's home address at that point if he knew it.

So, while Will and I were enjoying Mallory Square and Sunset, the two spiritual larcenists were driving up the Keys, intent on raiding my refrigerator and stealing our magic juice.

And the plot thickened...

Well, actually, I don't know if it thickened, but it certainly got more entertaining.

Both Miles and Constance had a weakness for mind-bending drugs like peyote and acid, generally combined with tequila. Although things rarely went well on those occasions, it was certainly entertaining, and this evening was no exception.

They were a little freaked out by having to rob someone. It

was just outside their comfort zone — but they weren't quite bothered enough morally to deny the process. So, they split a peyote brownie and a pint of tequila as they drove up the Keys to Big Pine, and found the location of my house via a local street map. They drove to the end of my street, parked, and casually walked back to my home, which was the last house before the mangroves that led to the bay. It was dark by this time and well after dinner, and no one in the few houses on my canal paid much attention. The two stayed within the shadows and made their way up the stairs to the deck and the front door.

Now normally, this wouldn't have gone well for them at all because of Shadow, my big German shepherd-Rottweiler mix, who had his own way of dealing with strangers, and Diego, who was staying with me. But Shadow was out on one of his wandering excursions with Jing's hawk, Cielo, and neither had made it home yet. And Diego was out on a dinner date with a local waitress.

It was an odd thing, but Shadow and Cielo had become remarkable companions and they often took off for hours, sometimes for the better part of a day and some of the night, exploring the mangroves and the undeveloped shorelines of the island.

Without too much trouble, the "reverends" jimmied the door lock (they had multiple talents aside from bringing out a chorus of hallelujahs from a congregation) and moved inside. Finding his way to the refrigerator, Miles dug around for a moment or two and came up with the laxative bottle with the strange-smelling liquid inside that definitely wasn't Ex-lax. He looked at his sister and smiled. Five minutes later, they were pulling out onto Highway 1.

The invasion of my home and the theft of the juice went much better than the two space ministers expected, and by the time they were back in Key West, Constance and Miles were seriously baked. They were high on success, tequila, and another half of a peyote brownie (which was really coming home now…

everything was taking on sort of a soft-yellow haze). It wasn't a bad feeling, it just wasn't great for making important decisions.

It was around this time that they decided they wanted to do a "test" for themselves before carrying this too much further. They just *had* to see if this stuff worked. (In their inebriated state, they were thinking "immediate" but of course, that wasn't quite the case with the magic juice.)

They were cruising down Duval Street, really loving the lights and the people and the brownie (especially the brownie) when they came to the Key West Butterfly and Nature Conservatory, which was pretty much a remarkable experience when you were straight... *But stoned, it be a whole 'nother thing, mon...* We're talking about hundreds and hundreds of colorful butterflies and beautiful tropical birds, all in an evening's calm, all across the domed enclosure, but prepared at any moment to release themselves in magical, multicolored waves, surrounding and lighting on the incredible tropical flora. It was the closest thing to Coiba Island you were going to get on mainland America. It was stunning, almost overwhelming to the average person. But right now, everything inside was quiet, tucked up, and just surviving the night, as most creatures do.

Given our funky evangelists and their present state of "zonk," they were just somehow smart enough to park the car, exit without falling, and work their way back to the butterfly conservatory. God knows how, but they somehow jiggled the backdoor lock and the door opened for them. (Possibly because the night watchman had gone out to get some coffee and forgot to lock it.) But that was pretty much the last gift the gods gave them.

"Oooohhh, man...where are the butterflies and birds?" mumbled Constance with glazed eyes as they stumbled cautiously into the huge room.

"Look, there...beautiful plants," slurred Miles, pointing at the huge, climate-controlled conservatory. "Freaking great place to test this stuff..." he muttered as he reached into his pocket and pulled out the bottle of magic juice.

Things basically went downhill from there.

Both of our ecclesiastical idiots had reached the "everything is just amazing" level often found with THC as they stumbled over and into the huge glass-enclosed conservatory/habitat with all the incredible flowers, plants, birds, and butterflies...most of which were dead still right now. Miles pulled the bottle of magic-grow juice from his pocket and just for fun, was splashing a little of it on the plants and the nearly tame birds. Part of him knew this wasn't a good idea, but another part of him just didn't give a shit. He was loving the strange colors…and the music (which only he could hear). They hadn't noticed the thousands of butterflies silently perched on branch and leaf with folded wings wrapped around themselves in nocturnal rapture.

It happened in an instant. Miles sneezed, sharply and abruptly. Suddenly, one pair of wings opened and burst into the air in a flutter, then another, and another…and a second later, there were thousands of furiously fluttering butterflies unfolding in multicolored waves, swinging up and out at them from the trees in a wild panic. This incited the birds, and instantly the interior changed into more waves of screeching, cawing creatures. Our wasted ministers screamed and stumbled toward the cage exit, certain that a colorful part of hell had come for them. In the process, Miles inadvertently tossed magic-grow juice everywhere. They stumbled through the conservatory, spilling juice on everything, not the least being themselves, butterflies, the birds, the plants, and the tile floors that had drains to the city water facilities. With the doors of the conservatory thrown open, it all became mayhem.

Not good at all…

The silent alarm had already gone off but it hardly mattered. The police found the two wasted, terrified intruders huddled in the corner of the main conservatorium covered in butterflies, and book-ended by a couple of macaws and a local raccoon. Their eyes were glazed and lost to any particular emotion, and drool ran down their chins.

Miles and Constance discovered later that getting the magic juice on your skin caused your hair follicles to go freaking nuts. It was now obvious that this "growth formula," while working most effectively on plants, had an effect on just about everything it touched. Inside of two days, Miles looked like a gorilla with mange. He had splotches of hair on his neck, face, arms, hands, and chest — everywhere the juice had splashed him. Miles had also managed to get the stuff on his sister's legs and arms, and she looked like a sheep.

In the following days, authorities described the incident as some sort of strange attack on Key West and the Nature and Butterfly Conservatory by a weird religious group who may or may not have been deranged nature haters. But they couldn't exactly explain the handful of butterflies the size of pigeons or the extraordinary plant growth throughout the building that spread into the sewer and water lines of Key West and exploded the local greenery in places. The city officials claimed it was possibly caused by a "rogue bloom" of some sort, which affected certain areas of flora and fauna around the island.

One thing for sure, our ministers of mayhem had lost their magic juice (with the bottle finally breaking on the tile floors of the Butterfly Conservatory). And both were just about furry enough to need dog tags. In addition, they were being held on numerous charges from breaking and entering and destruction of public property, to a half-dozen other allegations dealing with exotic wildlife injury and theft. The ministers were way out of business and reduced to praying for a miracle from their Bermuda Triangle gods…who were apparently busy elsewhere in the universe.

CHAPTER TEN

We weren't happy when we discovered that our half-bottle of Crazy Grow had been stolen from my refrigerator by a couple of deranged space ministers who then used it to "quick grow" the butterfly jungle in Key West. But we all really loved the photo in the *Key West Citizen* a couple of days later of the two somewhat fairly zoned perpetrators, who looked a little like yetis. Sometimes you get what you deserve…

There was absolutely no point in making a legal fuss about the theft from my house. All that would do was draw attention to us and we couldn't afford that right now. So we wrote it off. The best thing we could do was pull some more juice out of my safety deposit box and get the four ounces that were needed to the chemical analysis company, then wait for the results. Then we'd know which direction to take.

So, the following day I went to my bank and pulled out our second to last bottle of the magic juice and brought it home. Once there, Will and I measured out four ounces into a brand-new, medicine-type bottle and hid the remaining grow juice in my dirty laundry basket in the closet. That would have to do for now. We didn't feel like driving back into Key West right away, and we'd only be gone for a few hours.

The next day, Will, Diego, and I headed up to Miami. The meeting with the Organic Analysis Incorporated chemical analysis representative went smoothly. We offered very little information, other than the sample we provided was something we had found in an odd situation, and before we just poured it down the drain, we wanted to know what it was chemically.

It wasn't the guy's first rodeo. Carl had some experience

dealing with people who thought they might have something important…or not...and just wanted to know. Ninety-nine percent of the time it was nothing that significant. He was polite, informative, and even more neutral than we were pretending to be. Our new acquaintance in this process said he would need at least two weeks, maybe three. They were somewhat backed up and slightly understaffed right now.

We hid our disappointment, accepted his information, gave him the four ounces of juice, shook his hand, and left. There was nothing to do now but wait, and maybe that wasn't a bad thing. Because on top of all this, Will and I had developed an additional problem/situation. We were both beginning to feel like hell. It seemed like the flu — or at least, I hoped it was the flu. But we'd just gotten back from Central America, which was one of the breeding grounds for weird diseases for which they were only just finding names. It was like I was always tired and I couldn't seem to catch my breath, and my appetite was all but gone. Will felt exactly the same way.

We went to our doctor and he ran an extensive battery of tests but couldn't define it. And it wasn't going away. We were beginning to get worried, and so was our doctor. He recommended we try getting out of the Keys for a little while. Maybe some of this was psychological or maybe there was a local or indigenous element we were coming into contact with that was causing this. I told him we'd done that recently.

He said perhaps that was where the problem came from.

"What have you got to lose?" he said. "You've got the money, you've got the time. Get away, breathe some different air, try something enjoyable, and see if you feel better."

I have come to realize that there is good timing and bad timing, and the gods, they love to play with those intangibles. This was one of those times, and there's a story that goes with it.

That night, Will and I were having a couple of beers at the Green Turtle when we ran into an old friend. Rob Binson was a regular fellow, not one of the "gamblers" we knew, just a real estate agent who had done well in Key West. But he wasn't a happy man when we found him that evening. It turned out that his wife had contracted a virulent form of cancer six months ago and he lost her two months later. We offered our sincere condolences. He was a good guy and we hated to see that this had happened to him. Without any attempt at one-upmanship, we mentioned the health problems we were having.

"I swear to God I feel like I'm always out of energy," I said, commiserating. "I feel so rotten, I think this is the end. What a miserable way to go — tired, not hungry, not interested in anything. What's the point of staying around? Even the doctor won't rule out any possibility at this point." I paused. "I feel like it's the last hurrah."

"Same with me," muttered Will. "They haven't been able to pinpoint it, but the doc said there are several African/South American viruses floating around, and they don't talk about them much." He sighed. "Damn, I'd hoped to be having a better time than this at check-out time."

Will may have been talking a little figuratively (and we have a tendency to exaggerate some). We weren't at all sure we were dying. But our friend took us literally. He suddenly flashed a knowing if not melancholy smile, but with great understanding in his eyes.

"I know what you're going through," he said. "Believe me…" He paused as if coming to a decision, then offered a suggestion. "I know of just the place for you — both of you — when you sense your time is short…"

Then he took the next few minutes to tell us of an extraordinary resort off the coast of Jamaica.

"Everything you ever wanted," he said, his eyes lighting slightly with recollection. "The place was like magic — the most extraordinary, really enjoyable personal care you can imagine. It's very expensive, but if you want it, you can have it there. Anything. Anything you want." He paused. "It's called the Last

Resort. It's for people like you who have lived hard and well and want some…extraordinary time…for themselves." He exhaled softly. "Some magical time before the bell tolls…" He sighed. "I took my wife there, at the end — and it was the best, most remarkable experience…in a sense, for both of us."

The real problem with this conversation was a lack of communication. We didn't quite understand that his wife was dying when they left for the island, and he didn't understand that there was nothing identifiably cancerous or deadly wrong with us. We were just bitching about a freaking malaise we'd encountered, and we just sort of got our wires crossed — a byproduct of an afternoon of pot and tequila (and again, we have an inclination to exaggerate by nature).

So, the guy didn't quite get what Will and I were saying. He thought we were *really dying* (or at least one of us). And the place he told us about was the perfect place to spend the last of your time if you knew you were checking out and you wanted to have some control about it. It was a place designed to give you the greatest, ultimate experience when your time on this planet is finite and you know it. And most importantly, it was a resort that literally "checked you out of life." Yes…literally suddenly, painlessly, sometimes purely excitingly, checked you out, completely legally. With a contract… Maybe like…

One morning you're having a cocktail with your wife, watching the tennis players from the patio. You take a sip of your drink and suddenly, the few drops of strychnine in your orange juice hits. Kaboom! You're dead and your eyes are still watching the tennis game.

Or maybe…

Your wife has gone to bed early and you're finishing the rest of your cocktail at the bar when an absolutely drop-dead blond sits down next to you and strikes up a conversation. Inside of twenty minutes, you're up in her room stripped naked and having the wildest sex of your entire life when she subtly pops you with a hypodermic needle. You're gone just as you're getting off — you're coming as you're going...and suddenly, you're at the Pearly Gates. Hopefully...

(That part, no one could guarantee.)

Again, the problem was a lack of communication. We thought it was just the perfect resort where we could enjoy the ultimate in hedonistic pleasures for a short while — an "anything goes" type of place in hopes of getting out of a physical funk — that they probably supplied a variety of chemical, alcoholic, and companionship-type entertainment to keep you well beyond content. The truth was, we were both right and wrong.

So...being as bored and disappointed with life as we were at the moment, that evening Will and I discussed this Last Resort place, and you know, it sounded like maybe exactly what we needed — the ultimate in mind-numbing excitement and debauchery.

"If we're not getting any better, we might as well have some serious fun while we're dying," said Will with a sarcastic smile.

(*From the mouths of babes...*)

The following day, I found the phone number our friend had given us and made a call. Just for the hell of it. What did we have to lose?

The woman on the phone was somewhere between hot sultry and silky compassionate. They just happened to have a vacancy, as of last night... *Why don't we fly down and have a look? What did we have to lose?*

Diego would take care of Shadow, and Cody was already up and around now. Hell, we deserved some time off. After letting everyone on our team know what our plans were, we packed a couple of bags, hopped in Will's Cessna 310, and skipped across the Caribbean. We cleared Customs in Kingston, then headed to a small island on the southeast tip of Jamaica. "Serenity" it was called...

There was a cab waiting for us with a big Jamaican driver, who waved us over, grabbed our bags, and threw them into the trunk. "You headed to da Last Resort, right mons?"

We nodded.

"Yep," said Will. "Bring it on, give me your best shot."

The fellow looked at us a little strangely, then offered a hesitant smile.

That seemed odd...

One of the first things I noticed about the Last Resort was the fence. I'm talking a serious ten-foot chain-link fence that surrounded the entire ten acres. There were warning signs posted periodically mentioning its electrification, in sort of a nice way, like..."We want to keep you safe." But on the other hand, it certainly kept everyone out, or in, as well. As far as I could tell, there was only one way in and one way out of the whole complex — with a guard booth and an up/down rail gate across the road that looked like something from the Czechoslovakian border, and two armed guards.

"Quit freaking out and relax," muttered Will. "You're on vacation and these people are making sure it's a safe one."

When we arrived at the main building, we grabbed our bags and paid for the taxi. "See you on the flip side, mon," I said.

The fellow looked at me with that odd smile. "Dat's da spirit, mon. Don' you wish."

Once inside, we discovered that it was an extraordinarily beautiful resort. It was Caribbean picturesque in every fashion — magnificent, actually — with just about every convenience and entertainment you could imagine. The lady in charge, Madam Sharee Chaleen assisted us in completing the reservation for at least ten days...and helping us with the exorbitant amount of information regarding our physical and mental health history and finances. It seemed like a lot of information for a resort — bank accounts, banker's names, stocks and bonds, property owned... Actually, I'll admit I thought the info was overkill, and toward the end, Will and I just started initialing where we were supposed to and not concerning ourselves with the fine print. However, there were a few seriously unusual lines at the bottom of the questionnaire.

What is the designated cause of your...coming departure?

Your estimated expiration date...

I thought that was pretty strange...that maybe they were asking why we'd left the Keys. Foreign places often "mix" American sentences a little, so I wrote, *Maybe just plain boredom, nobody seems to know.* And as far as an expiration date, thinking they were speaking about the time frame of my stay, I joked, *Just not too soon, I hope, and not so long that I get bored...*

Madam Sharee also wanted to confirm that we both suffered from the same malady, and that our condition was in no way infectious. (We were required to bring a doctor's certification on that.) As far as we knew, there was nothing infectious about us. Finally, our hostess gazed at us with a combination of sweet empathy on one hand and hedonistic promise on the other. There was a strange melancholy about her, but there on the edges was a definitive gleam of promise and pleasure. She reminded me of a madam at an upscale bordello.

"You really are perfect for our small resort — just perfect," she said, offering another disarming smile. "You understand that whatever it is you're dealing with, whatever the physical or mental challenges you face, they will never be mentioned here on our premises. Never — from the moment you sign in, to the end of your stay." She held up a perfectly manicured finger. "It is a strict rule of the company — your time with us is to be entirely free of any sadness, remorse, or disappointment. Your time here with us will be the most incredible experience of your life...straight through to the last day. Painless, beautiful, exciting... The final, most wonderful hurrah."

Hmmmm...

I liked the incredible part but I wasn't quite sure what she meant about the "final hurrah" part.

But at the last moment, our host lost the Loni Anderson persona and got all Jane Fonda. She again held up a long, slender finger. "The only thing, the last aspect we must be clear about here, is that there is no reneging on this contract. Once you sign, the wheels of fate have begun to move, and the end of your journey, our relationship, and your payment are inevitable. A contract is a contract." And she stared at us. "This is important. Do you understand?" The lovely woman sighed but there was a strange heaviness about it. "We have a reputation to maintain…"

I shrugged and looked at Will. *Damn, it looked like these people were really insistent about keeping their image intact.* "We can live with that," I said.

Will shrugged too, then nodded.

Our host looked at me one more time and offered a genuine chuckle. "What courage and what an incredible sense of acceptance you have — humor at the gates of Heaven or Hell. You're both remarkable." She sighed softly. "You're obviously two people who know exactly who you are and the course you are set upon. Nothing is going to change that now." She smiled again. "I think we'll set you up for ten days plus, so we can have you around for a while. Okay? All we need now is the initial fifty percent deposit. Welcome to the Last Resort. Where there is hardly anything you can't have…until it's time to leave."

Five thousand dollars each, upfront…and five thousand more from each of us, to be withdrawn from our bank accounts in the Keys, "at the end of our stay..." It seemed like a lot of money but we were promised the experience of a lifetime and with all the unique treasures we had stumbled upon in our travels, money was not one of our problems. This was a drop in the bucket.

And so, our little jaunt in paradise began.

■ ■ ■

While we were experiencing this merry-go-round of confusion, and sincere, possibly terminal disappointment, back on the other side of the pond, technician Walter Hendricks of Organic Analysis Incorporated in Miami was in the process of an illuminating discovery or two. He read the initial analysis report and shook his head slightly. This was more of a preliminary analysis — a "meat and potatoes" report. The final investigative process would take several days yet, maybe a week. He'd run this again in the morning, just to be sure. If it came up the same, he'd contact Señor Jorgen before he showed his boss or anyone else. Señor Jorgen paid him well for "insight" on new things he stumbled upon. Besides, that man had a really bad temper, as the last head technician here could attest to…if he could…

It appeared that there was an element within this composite of recognizable components that was not homogenous, not easily identifiable. It wasn't to say that it might not be identified later, or that maybe it couldn't be copied in some fashion, but upon first examination, it was different, and this ingredient, in combination with the other more recognizable components, attacked the regenerative factors in plants and forced them (more like "chemically threatened" them) into mad reproduction. It had been proven before, in numerous studies around the world, that when the higher-consciousness entities (humans, animals, birds, and even some plants) were threatened in a wholesale fashion, there was often an instinctive drive to propagate. It appeared that this element was the chemical version of the physical drive to survive, and it was found in the product he was testing — in spades. In fact, this was a "kick your ass" super-buffered version.

He needed to run some more tests yet. But yeah, there was no question. Señor Jorgen was going to want to know about this.

CHAPTER ELEVEN

After we had settled into our spacious two-bedroom suite and unpacked, we called for room service, just for the heck of it. I ordered a filet minion and Will had the fresh lobster. In precisely fifteen minutes, our scrumptious meals were delivered by two knockout Scandinavian blonds. When we offered a tip, they politely refused, saying that gratuities were not necessary there. Then they stepped back, smiled seductively, and asked if there was anything else they could do for us.

Will looked at me, his mischievous eyes gleaming, then he turned to the girls. "Why don't you stick around for a while?" he said. "Maybe have a drink with us, and maybe we'll think of something."

The ladies grinned. "Our pleasure," they said in unison."

That evening was a great start to our "vacation."

It was a small but lovely resort. There were about a half-dozen beautiful Persian cats that roamed through the complex at will, and magnificent tropical birds, like macaws and yellow-naped parrots (some caged and some free) added to the ambiance. All of this blended with the high domed ceilings, terrazzo tiles, and a tropical atmosphere of palms, ferns, incredible flowers, and remarkable paintings.

There was a large outdoor pool and a smaller indoor pool, surrounded by a few private Jacuzzis. There were tennis courts, a horse stable, and bars about every fifty yards. There was also a selection of dune buggies for the more adventurous guests who wanted to see outside the resort (with a resort "guide" — *always with a resort guide)*. It was very close to Heaven here, for those who were on course for that particular paradise...*and had prepaid for the trip.* But the truth was, while the few patrons seemed fairly at ease in this somewhat bantam resort, there was an odd sense of almost too much "hurrah" — too happy, too frivolous, and too drunk at times.

There were maybe a dozen couples in the resort and a couple of individuals, which seemed a little strange. Most of the time it seemed as if everyone was enjoying their grand hurrah, but there was a part of me, as I watched the clients in the restaurants and pools and on the tennis courts, that caught a strangeness in their eyes — an odd introspection. Sometimes, as they stared out at the manicured grounds or swirled the swizzle sticks in their drinks, I noticed their eyes went distant and lost the "hurrah." And there were times, for just a moment, I would have sworn I saw apprehension, and maybe even desperation. It was damned unusual.

Nonetheless, there seemed to be a handsome man or woman everywhere to assist you in your own attempt at paradise. We woke up with a beautiful courtesan each morning, we played tennis after a breakfast fit for kings, then went sailing for a while on one of the house yachts — *with a resort guide...* We swam in the incredible pool, rarely without a drink in hand, and we danced with beautiful women until the lights in the ballroom dimmed.

It was an incredible week...except for maybe one thing. I noticed that people seemed to be disappearing. They didn't say goodbye, or it's been fun, they were just gone the next day.

The husband of a couple we had met on the tennis courts — a really nice guy — appeared to be enjoying himself, but he was one of the folks I caught with that look of apprehension. Then one day, he was gone. They said it was a heart attack when I asked. His wife left quietly the following afternoon and flew back to Chicago with his ashes.

When we offered our condolences before she left, the woman smiled strangely. "He's free now," she said. "No more pain…" She sighed. "No more anticipation…" Then she shrugged and offered a knowing smile. "We should all be so lucky."

What the hell was that about?

The following day, we lost another acquaintance — Tim Gilbert, a realtor from Dallas. A stroke, they said, while he slept. It was surprisingly convenient for a man who apparently suffered from the later stages of leukemia. Then there was a woman from Miami who disappeared later in the week. An aneurism, I heard, while shopping in the local village.

Over the next couple of days, I noticed that an oil baron from Texas — a guy name Ted Johnson — wasn't showing up at breakfast anymore. I inquired about him.

"Oohh, Mr. Johnson…" said our host with a cautious easiness. "He…*left*…the night before last."

"Headed home I guess," said Will.

The young man looked at us, a strange glint in his eyes. "Yes, you could say that…"

It wasn't that we weren't having a good time, but there was something just slightly out of kilter here. No one seemed particularly upset at the fact that people were dropping like flies in this place.

After about a week of this strange but remarkable time, Will and I were having breakfast one morning, when things got more definitive. The small breakfast room was nearly empty except for two couples near the entrance at the other side of the room, and a big Persian tomcat who had taken a liking to me. If we were in the main lounge or perhaps outside on the porch, he would come over and rub against me, offering an insistent "stroke me" purr (much like the courtesans we'd met there). I had just poured a fresh cup of coffee from our decanter when I noticed we were out of cream, so I asked the attendant close by (there was always an attendant close by) to bring us some fresh cream.

Moments later, she returned with a small open-faced decanter and set it down next to me. She looked at me strangely and said, "You have been a wonderful guest, and we have thoroughly enjoyed you."

There was something in her eyes that made me less than comfortable. I didn't really know why, exactly.

I returned to my conversation with Will. I wanted to finish the point I was making. But in the process, my Persian cat buddy smelled the cream and meowed insistently, rubbing against my leg. I chuckled at the audacity of all cats, pulled a saucer off the table, set it on the floor, and poured a little cream for the guy, then added some to my coffee. I was in a bit of a dialogue and didn't touch my beverage right away, but the cat went right to the saucer and lapped up what I had given him.

It took me a few minutes to finish the tale I was telling, and at the end, both Will and I were laughing. I was adding some sugar to my coffee, and Will was beginning to offer a counter-story. I had just brought up my coffee cup when the look on Will's face changed and he caught my hand.

"Hold on, buddy," he muttered cautiously, nodding to the cat that had been drinking the milk — the cat who was now lying on his side on the rug, his big, golden eyes wide and indifferent with death.

"That ain't right," Will said.

I looked around and noticed our two attendants exchanging glances. Then I turned to Will and his eyes said what I was thinking. Something was really bonkers here. There was a look on the faces of the waiter and the waitress that went from disappointment to ugly guilt.

"I think we'll skip breakfast," said Will, pushing back from the table.

"I think we need to see Miss Sharee Chaleen, now!" I growled, glancing around cautiously.

Five minutes later, we barged past Miss Sharee's receptionist — us and the dead cat — and were standing in front of Miss Chaleen's desk. Will tossed the cat onto the desktop.

The woman was surprised but not particularly shaken.

Will got right to the point. "What the hell is this place?" gritted my partner. "The elephant's graveyard?"

"I don't understand," said Miss Chaleen calmly. "Everything has been made perfectly clear to you from the very beginning."

"Yeah, we've had a great time," I sneered. "Except that people keep suddenly dying around us, and today it appears we've been added to the 'check-out' list."

Miss Chaleen shook her head and sighed like a school teacher dealing with a slow student. "You have paid for an extraordinary convenience for a while, and a final…*service*…all of which you are in the process of receiving." She held out her hands. "In real life, death is not always kind or quick, but it is here. That is what you have paid for. Plainly put, you came here to die, but with the kindest, most enjoyable prelude and passing possible. And we at the Last Resort offer a closing curtain quickly, without pain or consternation." Our hostess sighed. "It's what we agreed upon. It's what you paid for."

All of a sudden (I hate to say it) but the lights came on for both of us. I looked at my partner and he blinked a couple of times. Will turned slowly to Miss Chaleen like a man waking from a dream. "You mean everyone here is dying — and they know it, and they're paying you to check them out early, somewhere along the line…here? Like…surprise! You're dead!"

Sharee nodded. "Yes, of course, that's correct… It is the ultimate hedonistic experience. Death when you least expect it but when you need it. Painlessly, maybe even pleasurably…" She sighed again, a little frustrated. "I assumed you knew and understood all this. How could you not? You told me you had a friend whose wife was dying of cancer and stayed with us for a while."

Will and I looked at each other. *We had really crossed some wires here.*

She smiled at us. "We do sometimes keep some individuals with us longer than anticipated because of their personalities or the ambiance they add to our package, as we have with you two.

But very often it increases the anticipation, and that's not always good." Sharee paused. "So, last night we decided it was nearing 'the time' for you two." She looked at me. "We just happened to see a good opportunity this morning."

"Jesus Christ!" I cried. "We come here for a little relaxation and you want to freaking kill us!" I threw up my hands. "That's not relaxation to me by any stretch of the imagination."

"It's not our fault if you misread the purpose of our facilities," she said. "Now, you mustn't become a bother or I'll have to move you both up on the list—"

"Exactly how much more can you move us up?" I said sarcastically. "And what do you do with our bodies — just throw them in the ocean?"

"Oohh no, we wouldn't do something so crude," our hostess said. "We have our own cremation facilities —"

"Okay, okay, hold on here for a moment," Will said, holding out his hands. "Now, you understand that we're not dying. We never were. We just weren't feeling chipper. This is all a case of miscommunication. We're feeling better now. I think we just want a partial refund and we want to go home. *Now.*"

Our hostess shook her head. "Frankly, it doesn't matter to me if you're dying or you're not. You signed a contract, you availed yourself of our services for a period of time, and you led us to believe you were dying, so we intend to finalize our end of the bargain and collect the monies due us." She stared at us. "Do you think you're the first people in the history of our resort to change their minds?"

I stared, mouth open.

Will straightened up and took the reins again. "What? Are you mad? What crazy boat did you ride in on? You can't just kill people at your convenience, or because of a mistake in documentation."

"Yes, we can," Sharee said. "I have a contract. We here at the Last Resort have a reputation to uphold. We have never reneged on an agreement." She paused and held out a well-manicured hand. "The only exception is, if you pay us ten percent of your total wealth, you can leave alive. It's in the small print."

It was my turn again. "I don't care what's in the small print," I cried. "I'm not paying you shit, and I'm not dying at *your* convenience!"

Our host shook her head, unruffled by our rebuttals. "Unfortunately, you have to. We have a completely legal contract that allows us to...eliminate you...basically at our convenience. It's all signed by you and notarized. It's not our fault that you've miraculously recovered."

"I should have taken a little more time with that freaking contract," hissed Will, reading my mind.

"We were never...freaking...dying!" I yelled. "How hard is it to get that through your bloody head?"

"Small print," Miss Chaleen said again. "Read the small print, dear sirs. If you attempt to leave here without your contracts being fulfilled, you are liable for ten percent of your primary bank accounts and the Last Resort, Inc. is legally permitted to fulfill our contract of termination at any time thereafter. Period."

She paused and any nice that existed in her melted away. Our hostess exhaled and casually pressed a button on her desk. Almost instantly, two huge dudes (linebackers in slacks and tropical shirts) appeared from a side door.

"We'll give you a couple of hours to think it over," she said. "To come to your senses and accept the kismet you designed. Or accept the conciliatory payment to us." She paused and offered a smile. "Death isn't really all that bad. It's just one door closing and another opening."

"Easy for you to say," I muttered angrily.

The two heavies escorted us to a two-bedroom apartment — not ours, they weren't taking any chances — and one fellow stayed outside the door. (I checked.)

The truth was, Will and I were left in an almost stunned

state. It all seemed like some sort of incredibly bad joke. I kept waiting for our realtor friend in Key West to come through the door laughing and offering a "gotcha!" The whole thing was like a terrible dream.

"Now I understand the twelve-foot-tall fences around everything and all the security personnel," I grumbled.

Will looked at me. "Maybe we should pay them, huh?"

I shook my head. "No, man. You know how much ten percent of our wealth is? It's like extortion — like the mob!"

"Yeah, but on the other hand, there's dead," said Will. "Like *dead.* No breathing. That's a little too final for me."

"I think they're bluffing. No business in this day and age chases you down and kills you if you don't pay a bill."

"Famous last words," huffed Will. "You want to risk that being found on your tombstone?"

I exhaled slowly and glanced around. "We need to find a way out of here."

My partner nodded. "Ya, mon. Right you are. Time to slip out the back, Jack."

I smiled. "And make a new plan, Stan…"

CHAPTER TWELVE

Time was not on our side. Time is never really on anybody's side, but in this case, we were really behind the curve. There was the one-time payment of ten percent of our combined wealth, which would get us out of this. But man, that was nothing more than blackmail and it really grated me. Stupidly, we had signed a non-litigation release in the original package, so they didn't really care about that. I figured that likely, our number was up regardless of what we paid. In the business these folks ran, the most satisfied customer was a dead customer.

I turned to Will. "We need to act fast. The longer these folks have to think about this, the more of a liability we become."

Will nodded soberly. "And they've already got the documents that give them permission to snuff us."

I glanced around the room. "We need a way out of here…" I repeated.

"I'll click my heels," muttered my partner.

I looked up at the large air conditioning vent in the ceiling, then walked over to the walk-in clothes closet. I discovered a number of women's dresses in the very back, and a few hats and scarves — apparently the possessions of a former client…who probably didn't need them anymore. I pulled out a couple of dresses.

"I've got a better idea," I said, looking at my friend. "I'm betting you're probably a nine or a ten." I held out a dress. "This one should work for you."

"This is no time to be getting kinky on me," said Will, holding up a finger and shaking it.

"Trust me, okay?"

"Yeah, great. The last time I heard you say that there were two hookers and a bottle of tequila involved... You remember how that ended?"

"Nobody's perfect, okay? Just slip on your dress, Sally, and we'll see if we can't find you some lipstick."

Will shook his head. "Man, this is going downhill fast..."

Ten minutes later, we looked like a couple of fairly ugly but somewhat acceptable women (as long as no one looked too close). We found a small carryall and Will stuffed our real clothing inside while I pulled a clothes bureau underneath the AC vent in the ceiling and worked the screws out of the frame with my pocketknife. A few moments later, Will shoved me up into the narrow airway, then tossed up the carryall and followed.

Sure enough, the air conditioning ductwork led to the next suite in the complex. We bypassed that one (too close to our room), then crawled down a ways. Will kicked out the vent in the next suite and we dropped down into an empty room. We straightened our dresses and our hats (which helped cover our faces), then, standing by the door, we surveyed each other for a moment.

"Damn, you're an ugly woman," Will said with a grin.

"Yeah, well, you're no prize either," I replied.

We paused for a second.

"We need a distraction now," my buddy said.

I agreed as we looked around.

Will stopped and stared at the fire alarm switch on the wall. "That'll work."

I nodded, slipped back the glass covering, and pulled the lever.

A moment later, we stepped out into the hall to the clanging of the fire alarm. After offering a quick wave at the resort heavy guarding our door down the hall, we quickly moved away. I could feel the guy's eyes on us. I kept waiting for the shout but he was busy now, banging on the door to our suite. Nonetheless, I'm pretty sure I heard the guy mutter something about "really ugly broads."

Will instinctively started to turn on the insult but I grabbed his arm. "Let it pass, mama," I whispered. " 'Cause you do be a homely bitch..."

Five minutes later, we had made it out of the lobby doors with a rush of clients and employees, and into the sunlight of the outer fenced courtyard. We looked like two hairy-legged, feminine train wrecks, but no one cared right now. The word "fire" has a way of making people pretty damned myopic.

But now we needed some transportation. We had to get through the complex gate and make it about a mile down the road to the little corporate airstrip, where Will's 310 was waiting. I pointed over at the golf carts. One of those would do just fine.

The gate to the complex had been thrown open to allow the island's fire department truck to get through. We just hopped into a cart, tossed the carryall into the back, cranked it up, and disappeared out the gate. In less than ten minutes, we were at the little airstrip and buckling up in the 310. With little more than a "Hi-ho, Silver!" we were in the air and headed home.

Within the hour we had refueled in Kingston and set our course for the Keys.

■ ■ ■

The panic had been quelled at the Last Resort, and Miss Sharee Chaleen was pissed to spitting BBs. There was really no damage to the complex. The damage lay in her pride. No one had ever done anything as dramatic as this before. Oh, there had been those who had changed their minds at the last minute. But that hardly made any difference. *A contract was a contract.*

She was one angry woman but she was going to fix it. Yes, she was...

Miss Chaleen turned to her secretary. "Get me the Twins on the line. Tell them we've got a runner — two runners..."

By the time we had made our quick fuel stop in Kingston and were headed across the small international air corridor over Cuba, Miss Sharee was arranging a meeting with a couple of unique individuals. Their occupation — profession, if you will — was locating and most often convincing people to return what they had taken or pay what they owed. It was amazing how many people/organizations had folks who were hiding from them. But the truth was, most of the Twins' clients weren't so much concerned with conciliation. The better part of the time it was just debt payment and revenge, and the Twins were good at revenge. Actually, they specialized in it.

They were two individuals who truly enjoyed their work. After all, it was like a remarkable game of hide and seek…

■ ■ ■

It was a long flight but finally, we were slipping down onto Runway 27 at Key West International. It had been a strange adventure — interesting and odder than most — and I was glad to be home. As we unloaded our gear and tied down Will's plane, I was looking forward to a couple of days of nothing. I hoped that our affiliation with Miss Sharee Chaleen and her Last Resort was over. But I wasn't sure of that.

One of the good things out of all this was that the physical malaise Will and I had dealt with before our visit to the resort seemed to have mostly dissipated. It was hard to say why — maybe a different environment, or maybe all the interesting times and lovely ladies. Regardless, I was looking forward to a little relaxation. But there was still the magic juice to deal with, and we would have felt considerably less comfortable if we'd known about the Twins.

■ ■ ■

While we were settling in at our respective homes (my house on Big Pine Key and Will in his converted shrimp boat in Key

West), Miss Sharee was meeting with two folks who were intent on changing our lives. She was giving them photos, addresses, phone numbers, and instructions regarding a failure to cooperate on our part. The Twins didn't need much instruction on the last issue. Getting cooperation out of people was another of their specialties.

■ ■ ■

Will called the team and let them know we were back. We'd been gone the better part of ten days, and there was still a major issue at hand regarding our magic-grow juice. There was a chance the chemical analysis company might have some news for us by now. Will and I called our kids as well — Tax and Jing — and made plans to see them the following day.

The next day, while I waited for Will to come over, I called the chemical analysis people in Miami. As it turned out, they *did* have some news for us, but the fellow we'd spoken to earlier was damned closed-mouthed about it and wasn't interested in answering any questions over the phone. He recommended we come up to the company facilities as soon as possible — like, tomorrow. There was little choice. I told him we'd be there the following afternoon. But when I hung up, I realized we'd made plans to meet with Tax and Jing.

Will just shrugged and said, "Bring 'em along. We can talk on our way to Miami and have lunch together afterward."

I figured this would be easy enough. But then I should have remembered what our old Rastaman buddy, Rufus, had to say about the gods and their desire for "complicated entertainment."

Speaking of gods and entertainment…

■ ■ ■

While I was calling the chemical analysis company in Miami, Flight 661 from Jamaica was arriving in Key West. The two individuals known as the Twins were just debarking.

Strangely enough, most everyone just kind of stepped aside and made room for them as they worked their way off the aircraft. Some folks just have that effect on people…

■ ■ ■

The following day at about one o'clock, we arrived at Organic Analysis Incorporated in Miami. I picked a spot in the parking lot and we stared at the sizable office building. Tax and Jing stayed with the car while Diego, Will, and I headed into the building. It was a cool day, and frankly, this was one of those things where smaller was better.

Once inside, we walked across the terrazzo floor and announced ourselves to an attractive secretary, who made a call from the switchboard. She looked up and smiled. "Second floor, room 207."

Room 207 seemed to be partly lab and partly a small reception area. One sort of bled into the other. After a moment or two, we were greeted by a little guy obviously affiliated with the chemical analysis part (white lab coat, slacks, and tennis shoes). But there was also a fellow with longish dark hair, a swarthy complexion, and hard, dark eyes, trying to appear casual but not succeeding as he stood by the window. There was an ugly air about him — not much conscience in those eyes. There were also two big guys within quick reach of him — bodyguard types with crew cuts, large shoulders, cold eyes, the remaining scars of teenage acne, possibly brothers. One was over by the door, and one was sitting in a nearby chair.

After a very brief introduction to the boss-like fellow, Mr. Tenseno (there was no intro to the big guys), the chemist cleared his throat and spoke.

"I'll get right to the point. What you have here…" he cleared his throat again. "Let me put it in terms you'll understand. Some of the elements in this formula we recognize and can reproduce, but the truth is, this is a little like apples and oranges…and golf balls." He paused. "We know about apples and oranges and we can blend them, but we can't blend them with golf balls. It doesn't generally work." He sighed. "Let me put it another way. This stuff you brought us…the chemical and elemental analyses for this stuff are literally out of this world. While we understand some of it, we would struggle to reproduce this, at least at this point. The truth is, we need a lot more to run tests on it." He paused again. "Where did you get this?"

"Someplace far away," I said without any commitment.

"You got more?" said the swarthy guy standing by the window.

I didn't see the point of lying at that moment. "One more bottle."

The chemist fellow eased out a frustrated sigh and glanced at his big companions.

The guy by the window stepped forward. The man looked at us and his face went from the professor's assistant to hitman. "We want it," he said. "And we want the formula."

"There is no formula," I cried, holding out my hands. "We told you that earlier. Why the hell do you think we're here? We found this shit in a cave in the jungle of Central America."

The two guys in front of us shared a glance. The boss man turned to me. "Is there more of this?"

Will looked at me, then turned to the guy. "We don't know. Honestly. We don't know. Could be…"

Diego stepped in closer.

The boss man's eyes went hard and his people suddenly reached inside their coats.

"Wait," said Diego, holding up a hand. "Wait…es possible there may be more." He turned to look at us. "We really didn't check. We were in a hurry. There could have been other… closets…" He turned back to the obvious boss man and held out his hands. "Es possible, amigos…" Then he turned to us again. "Why make a place like that for a handful of flasks? Es more likely it was maybe a place to store or distribute of some sort, eh?" He shrugged and attempted a disarming smile. "Maybe... eh?"

The boss man stepped in again and shook a finger at us. "So, you go to wherever the hell it is that you found this shit and bring us all you find...you understand?"

"No one is gonna order me back into that jungle so I can give whatever I find to them," I growled. "*You* understand?"

The largest of the two bodyguards sighed angrily and stared at us. "Okay, enough screwing around. You know the two youngsters you had watching your car?"

Will and I exchanged a worried glance.

"They're not there anymore," he said. "We have 'em."

I started to lurch forward. Will yelped in shock and stopped me. He stepped over to the window, looked at the parking lot, and his face paled.

"What do you want?" my friend said. He turned and repeated coldly, "What...do...you...want..."

"Simple," said the swarthy guy. "We want all of that particular formula you have — all you can find. We put a tap on your phone yesterday." He paused. "And we know you have some in the bank."

I cringed. Shit! I had mentioned that to Will yesterday while on the phone. I was subtle and the average person wouldn't have understood, but they had figured it out.

"You get all you have together for us. We want that tomorrow, delivered here." Then his eyes went hard. "You got a week on the other thing, in Panama. Otherwise, we give you your people back in pieces. *Capiche?"*

We were screwed three ways to Sunday and we knew it. Will and I shared another glance, then my partner spoke.

"Okay, you win. But give us the kids and we'll make a trip back into the jungle."

"I don't think so," said the big guy with a sly grin. He paused for a moment in thought. "I tell you what. We'll give you one of them. One is as good as two in this case, and less hassle for us. But first, you give us all that damned 'grow shit' stuff you have. We keep one kid until you get back from Panama." He paused and his face went hard. "And you'd better find more…"

The implication was loud and clear.

One of the heavies went downstairs and brought the kids up, so we could explain and they could choose. Ultimately, gallantry and necessity won out. Tax insisted that they free his sister. He wouldn't talk about it past that. He was set as hard as stone. He had spent his entire life protecting Jing and he wasn't going to fail her here by leaving her a prisoner to a chemical company and the mafia. And ultimately, Jing and her hawk were an asset in any uncertain situation. And this was going to be another damned uncertain situation.

■ ■ ■

When the meeting concluded between the mafioso, the chemist, and us (and Will, Diego, Jing, and I had reluctantly left the building), there was one last incident that we were not aware of involving Travis Christian and his damned proactive nature. No one had any idea that he had followed us up to Miami. A lone mission, you might say…

One of the big bodyguards went down on the elevator to get the car. The other one and the boss, along with Tax, took the next one down, a few minutes later. But when the elevator doors opened, there was no car and no other bodyguard. There was just a huge man with longish dark hair and hard green eyes standing in front of them. Before anyone really put it all together, Travis stepped in and popped the mafia bodyguard in the throat with a knuckled hand — hard. The man's eyes went wide and his hands instinctively went to his throat, which left a lot of his body unprotected. In one powerful motion, Travis kicked him in the groin and when the fellow dropped to his knees, our huge friend hammered him with a heavy right that buried him in the corner of the elevator.

Before the mafioso leader could draw a breath, Travis grabbed him and slammed him into the corner, and almost as if by magic, a KA-BAR knife appeared in our friend's hand. Travis grabbed the man's hair and jerked his head back, then laid his knife on the man's cheek and drew a red line down it.

"I belong to a very special club," he growled, his face almost touching the mafioso's. "You come back at me — you hurt that boy or any of my people, three more just like myself will come for you."

With that, he brought the blade down to the man's jugular and pressed sharpened steel against flesh. There was a definite quiver from the boss man as he gasped, eyes wide with terror.

"Do you really want that kind of karma?" hissed Travis. "Do you?"

There was a slightly audible, "No," in response.

"I'll let you have your 'security' here but if you hurt that boy in any fashion, if I hear he was just uncomfortable," hissed Travis, "I'm coming back for you and you won't believe what I will do to you, even as it's happening." Travis turned to Tax then, and suddenly, his face lost its intensity. He reached out and affectionately patted the young man's cheek. "Stay strong," he said with a smile. "I'll be back for you, I promise."

The truth was, Travis could have probably forced the issue there and made them return Tax, but it would have made for one more confrontation, possibly serious, that could have gone bad and disrupted the mission. Aside from that, Travis had a particular affection for Tax. The youngster reminded him a great deal of himself when he was young and stupid. Most importantly, there was that old feeling stirring in him that said this was going to be a damned uncomfortable affair in Panama. *That was one less life he had to worry about...*

■ ■ ■

We returned home that evening and called for a meeting of the team. We would gather at Eddie's at noon the following day.

The bad guys were right — all we had of the magic formula was half a bottle in my laundry basket and a bottle in my safety deposit box. I went to my bank the following morning, then Will and I drove up to Miami and reluctantly surrendered the remainder of our magical chemical. It wasn't worth Tax's life in any way, shape, or form.

We did, however, manage one concession. It was agreed by everyone that it was better if there was quality control on the storage of the full, unopened bottle. I explained that the bottles had been held in a controlled-environment vault at my bank. For the safety and the quality of the last full bottle, it would be better left stored at the chemical facility, along with the half-bottle.

The mafia guy wasn't happy about that but the little chemist agreed with us wholeheartedly. I could see he was terrified that these mafia cretins would do something to ruin the formula. So, in the end, all the juice we had — one and one-half bottles — stayed at the facility.

Then we returned home. This new jaunt wasn't going to be fun or enjoyable in any fashion. It was all a purely dangerous endeavor. We had to return to an island that would be on guard for intrusion (because of our last episode there), then work our way through the jungle to a hidden cave and hope, just hope, that there might be more "Blood of the Gods" to be found. And not spill any of our own blood in the process.

CHAPTER THIRTEEN

By the time the majority of the Hole in the Coral Wall Gang got to Crazy Eddie's Bar and Swill, the sun was near to setting. We gathered in the back room and closed the door to the bar. Cody was there as well. He was up and around now and doing well, but not well enough for a gig like this. Still, it was good to see him. It was as much a war council as it was an embarkation on another adventure this time. One of our people was being held — my son. Where, we didn't know, and we didn't have time to try and find him and take him back. We had to make Coiba Island and the grow juice our priority.

Travis looked around the table, those big green eyes filled with fire again. He was in his element. "We'll use the small island of Jicaron off Panama as our staging base again," he said. "We do this one just like a military mission." He eased out a breath and looked over at Eddie. "You take us in with the Goose, to Jicaron in the evening. The following morning at sunrise, you take us to Coiba Island. We'll use a neutral engine approach and a dead-stick landing. Same spot as last time. One team takes the target while a backup team covers the perimeter, and someone watches the plane." Our big friend glanced around at the rest of us. "Eddie, you stay with and watch your aircraft. Be ready to lift off in a heartbeat."

Eddie nodded and adjusted his black eye patch — a reflexive thing I'd noticed he did every time we were going into the fray.

Travis drew a breath and continued. "The primary team going in has to be the people who know the target — Kansas, Will, and Diego." He looked at us. "Your job is to get to the mission target without engaging anyone, if at all possible. Find the cave and search it thoroughly. You know what you're looking for. The backup/protectionary team will be Jing and me. We'll position ourselves to cover your flanks and watch the path coming into the target area. Supposedly, there are damned near thirty prisoner camps on this island, so we need to be careful. Everyone will have a radio. *Everyone.* We'll choose the frequency as we go in."

Travis wasn't asking, he was telling. He fixed his gaze on Jing. "I want you to bring your hawk in with you. I've seen that creature in action. It's almost like he has a sense of danger, and we need every angle we can get. Are you good with this?"

"You bet," she said. "And you're right, he sees and hears things way in front of us."

Everyone nodded. It all made sense. Besides, few people knew danger and war like Travis, with the exception of Cody. I could tell having to sit this one out made Cody crazy. I could see it in his eyes, but he knew, given his condition, how easily he could become a liability.

Travis took another look at all of us. "We saddle up at dawn, at the company hangar in Key West. Again, everyone will have a portable radio. The base station will be the one in the Goose. Dress for the jungle and war…with the weapons of your choice." He paused and eased out a sigh. "And pray to God you don't have to use them."

That night there was little sleep for any of us. We were going back into a place we had narrowly escaped just weeks before, the prison from hell. And the contingent of guards and soldiers there, not to mention the warden, would be on guard. We had beaten them once at this game, by nothing more than luck and the arrival of a weird and timely companion by the name of Archo Coco. Now we had to do it again. And mixed somewhere in all this was the Last Resort and the rancor of Miss Sharee Chaleen.

Speaking of the devil…there was one odd exchange for me before I called it a night.

After our war meeting at Eddie's, we all made our way home for what little sleep the gods would grant us. I was just outside of Key West, crossing Big Coppit Key and heading up to Big Pine when I stopped to get a six-pack at the local convenience store. I needed to back off some of the anxiety if I was going to sleep tonight. The vehicle behind me pulled in too but I didn't give it much thought. A Chevy van… It pulled over to the side and the lights went out as I climbed the stairs to the store.

I was in line to pay for my Coronas when two fairly attractive blonds — nice figures but not knockouts, white shorts, and tropical-looking blouses — came through the doors of the PicNic store. Tourists, most likely, and they looked like they were definitely very close to being twins. And I liked twins…

One of them looked at me and offered a bit of a "come hither" smile. I thought at the time, *If I wasn't in the midst of a "situation"…*

But she didn't let it go. "Beautiful evening," she offered. "Nice night for a couple of beers and a walk on the beach…"

It was a little strange. I mean, I'm not a bad-looking guy, and I'd had my share of impromptu liaisons, but this inference seemed… rushed.

I agreed with a smile and moved forward in line. As I paid for my beer, I glanced up at the shiny round client observation mirror and caught them behind me, exchanging a look. The slightly taller one smiled almost imperceptibly.

When I got outside and almost to my car, I took a deep breath. The two ladies came out behind me and the taller one spoke.

"Hey, fella… You with the beer and the nice eyes…"

(Hmmm…compliments now…)

"Do you know of a place around here, a quiet place, where a girl could drink a beer and stare at the moon a little?"

There was something about this whole thing that was setting off my internal alarms — that unique part of my psyche that had kept me alive all these years. Or maybe I was about to wake up from this dream, sweaty and disappointed.

I held up my hands. "Ladies, ladies…I appreciate the offer but I've got a schedule I've gotta keep, places I have to be, and as much as I'd like to spend some time with you…staring at the moon…I'm going to have to pass."

I backed up a little, just to get a little distance between us, and put my hand on my truck's door handle.

My two new friends glanced at each other, appearing more disappointed than the situation warranted. The one closest to me suddenly reached into her purse and the other one looked like she just wasn't going to take "no" for an answer. *This didn't feel right…*

At that moment, there was a roaring and clanking coming in off the highway, and an older van decorated with peace signs and Woodstock slogans came bouncing off the road and into the parking lot, almost tumbling to a halt in front of the PicNic store.

The girls in front of me, hands still at their big purses, slowed, their eyes talking hesitation and disappointment as the door of the Woodstock van swung open and a tallish, skinny Jamaican with coco-colored skin and ebony dreadlocks falling to his shoulders stumbled out. He straightened up, looked around, and when he saw me he offered a huge, toothy-white smile.

"Kansas! Kansas from de Big Pine Key! By the gods and the stars and all the tiny fish in the sea! What a coincidence, mon!"

Rufus! Lord! It was Rufus, our strange Rastaman witchdoctor-cum-purveyor of past and future, and a fellow of remarkable timing. He threw out his arms and lurched at us like something out of the *Mummy's Revenge*, a pint of cheap rum in one hand and a doobie in the other. I was reminded once again that there was no such thing as coincidence when it came to our impossibly remarkable friend, who was attuned to the stars, the wind, the sea, and things that the rest of us can't even see.

The women next to me stared in disbelief at Rufus, then they looked at each other.

"Another time, maybe," said the tall one, obviously put off

by the additional company.

Without another word, they turned and were gone, the red taillights of their car marking their disappointment…and maybe mine as well.

But truthfully, I wasn't sure whether I was disappointed or strangely relieved. It seemed as if I had just escaped a situation, and I wasn't sure what kind...

My old friend, Rufus, stopped and stared at me. Much of the façade of inebriation fell away but the bouquet of hashish enveloping him still remained like the cloud around Charlie Brown's gritty companion, Pigpen.

I shook my head. "Timing is everything, man…" I sighed. "But then, you know that."

"I been hearing rumors dat maybe you and Wilmon been dancin' with da devil again," Rufus said, his head cocked slightly.

I shrugged. "Yeah, I guess so. Had a recent adventure in Jamaica. Always read the fine print…" I eased out another sigh. "Off to Panama tomorrow — another story, with a good ending, I hope."

Our Rastaman friend nodded as if I was telling him something he didn't already know. "I be very glad to find your acquaintance again, and to see that your breathing apparatus still functions well." Then Rufus paused, his eyes narrowed, and he became a more serious version of himself. "But you know, breathing well can be a very tentative thing, and sometimes in da book of life, der is only a single page between breathing and not breathing…"

"Yeah," I said with a sage nod. "Been there…"

"So you have," my gangly friend muttered. "So you have…" He sighed as if coming to a decision. "I maybe have a small gift for you today."

I tilted my head in question, both curious and concerned because if Rufus gave you a gift, it was usually because you were going to need it.

"Do I need it?" I asked boldly.

Rufus shrugged. "Maybe, maybe not. It be a very simple gift."

As I stood there, Rufus reached into the pocket of his shorts and came out with something. He opened his hand and in his palm was a coin — what looked like a very old, possibly silver coin, a little too tarnished to be certain, slightly larger than a quarter. He handed it to me and I took it, studying the design — very likely Roman or Phoenician or something like that. Maybe older, for all I knew. It had the image of a beautiful woman's face on one side (the design was extraordinarily detailed and attractive), and the image of a hideous-looking coiled serpent on the other. *Heads a beautiful woman, tails a terrible serpent...*

"There is a thing about this coin," my friend said. "It always lands tails up, showing da snake, no matter who flips it or how hard it is tossed or whatever it is thrown against. It always lands showing the snake." He paused. "Well, maybe once in, say, every thousand tosses it might go to heads, maybe." He shrugged. "But I wouldn't worry 'bout dat. Da gods would have to be in a very strange mood. But never rule anything out. Because impossibility and coincidence are da god's favorite wine, and dey got a wicked sense of humor."

It didn't take much to see the potential for something like this, but it seemed a little...impossible. After all, it was just a coin.

"It's *not* just a coin," said Rufus, reading my mind. "It was made a thousand years before the first stones on the walls of Rome were laid, mon. It was created by people who understood time and the elements in fashions we have yet to conceive." He pointed to the coin. "This is not a gift. It is a loan. It has other journeys to make."

I cautiously thanked my most unusual friend, and carefully put the coin in my pocket, certain now that risky times might well wait around the corner.

But what a unique gift, if it actually worked...

We spoke for a few moments about journeys we had made recently, things in the past and maybe things to come, then Rufus paused.

"It is good to have envisioned your acquaintance again, old traveler," he said, then he sighed. "Well, I have some road to travel tonight. You not de only fishes in dis sea of confusion."

Then, with a final, cautious smile, he was in his van and gone, and I was by myself, standing in the parking lot of a ratty convenience store brushed by the last wafts of Rufus' ganja. An old yellow moon was rising behind me, witnessing another night of the perpetual foolishness of men and women, and all their adventures on this green ball of dirt and water.

I looked at the coin, then flipped it into the air and it came twirling down and slapped the ground, tails (the snake) up. I did it one more time with the same result. Then I walked over to the convenience store and threw the coin against the wall. The ancient money piece tumbled across the pavement and stopped in front of me like an obedient dog, snake up. Then I just dropped it. Snake up. "Damn…" I whispered as I picked it up and put it in my pocket. "Damn…"

■ ■ ■

Only a moment or two later, as both Rufus and I pulled out of the convenience store parking lot headed in our predisposed directions, two people exited from the van that had turned in behind me earlier and parked in the shadows of the tall oleander bushes near the highway. Both of the occupants — a man and a woman — appeared to be Asian. The guy was smallish, maybe five foot five, with dark, shoulder-length hair and strange, almost green eyes that were rarely still. His name was Quan. The woman was very similar in features to the man. She possessed the same controlled movement and her skin was the same soft amber, but her dark hair fell nearly to her waist and she was taller, slender, and tightly muscled, like a dancer. There was something sensual and jeopardous about her at the same time. Her name was Tranga. Last names were not important. They changed them often in their business.

But their most startling and unusual characteristic was their faces. The two shared the exact same face — the same eyes, nose, and mouth...as if they had been cookie-cutter stamped by God. But their eyes carried little or no emotion, like a mannequin's. While they weren't twins exactly, their voices, appearance, expressions, and movements were eerily alike. They were like one person in two bodies.

While they both possessed a variety of talents, they would have probably described themselves as "people who found people who didn't want to be found." They specialized in contracts and bones, working for those who needed one or the other finalized or broken. Their ancestors were a cunning, cautious, and clever breed, having survived the jungles of Southeast Asia for a thousand years, and the art of the hunt was in their blood.

But as Rufus would tell you, *"It don' matter who you are or what you are. If the gods are bored, you be nothing but entertainment..."*

And unfortunately, Quan and Tranga were about to find that out.

The final oddity was their mutual Caribbean brogue. While born overseas in Southeast Asia, they were raised from infancy in the Caribbean — Jamaica, actually. They'd been on the streets of Kingston since they were old enough to walk, and that harsh, unsparing environment had taught them the final necessity in their work. *Conscience was a luxury for people who could afford it.* By and large, they had grown up without any such thing.

"Well, dat with da women did not work," muttered Quan in his island brogue (which seemed out of place coming from his lips). "Something be wrong to da fellow. Or maybe he jus' don' like women."

"Maybe it be," replied his companion in the same brogue.

"But dere be no point in chasing dese geese tonight. Dat mon and his people, dey be going somewhere, brother. Dey meet in the bar, whisper with hard eyes, and study maps." She nodded sagely and held up a finger. "Now I be curious about this. I think patience and timing be the parents of success here. Maybe we wait for dem to come back, brother. There are worse places to spend some days."

Her companion shrugged. "I think we should jus' kill him and his friend and go home. Chaleen say she be okay with that."

And in truth, they probably should have because the next morning, by the time they got around to checking my house and Will's houseboat, we were long gone — soaring across the blue-green Caribbean Sea in Eddie's big Goose. The only thing that greeted them at my place was a huge dog (Shadow) and my drop-dead gorgeous blond neighbor, and neither offered much in the way of information.

But then, the two inquiring weren't exactly new to the challenges of locating people, and when they explained that they were old friends of ours from the Bahamas in town for a few days and hoping to tie up, our neighbor offered a little more than she should have, like Panama and an island called Coiba, and that we'd be back in a week.

■ ■ ■

Once again we "jumped the pond" to Cancun, where we spent the night. Then, the following day, we headed down to southern Panama and the Santa Catalina Airport. We found lodging at a local motel where we'd stayed before, then laid out our battle plans. Travis had given Will a special role on this mission. He wanted to know what we were up against regarding the island personnel, the stone fortress, and the terrain of the island itself. The flora and fauna, the locations of the more significant *desperadatos* camps, and who actually managed it all. (The name for the island prisoners — *desperadatos* — was a bastardization of Spanish and indigenous Indian terms that seemed to have stuck over the years.)

What was the name of the man in charge? Who was he? And were there any weaknesses? Will did his usual thorough job, touching civilian and military authorities here and there, then reported back.

At that point, our team checked our gear and weapons, (everyone carried light semiautomatic rifles, and pistols, knives of choice, and a radio). And Jing had her magnificent hawk, Ceilo. *A Doberman with wings...*

Then we went over the approach once more. We'd come in from Panama to Jicaron Island tomorrow afternoon aboard the Goose. The following morning, just before sunrise, we'd make our move to Coiba Island. We had no time to dally, no room for mistakes. My son was being held for ransom by some sort of Miami mafia, and we had to get this part right — which included making it to the cave in question and hopefully, locating more of the magic juice. I refused to think negatively on anything beyond that.

Watching Travis through all this, I marveled at the raw umbrage he possessed for someone taking one of his people — his family, I'd come to realize. All I knew for sure was, I wouldn't want to be one of those Miami mafiosi when we got back and had Tax in our possession.

■ ■ ■

We couldn't have known but this whole affair was about to be made a good deal more challenging by a fellow named Colonel Martino Jallente. The good colonel was the commandant of the Coiba Penal Island and Prison, and it just so happened that he was pissed at the world right now, regardless of the strange, recent invasion of his island.

This had not been a good month for Señor Jallente. Actually, it had been a while since he'd had a good month.

When the commandant found out what had happened — how his people and his system had failed earlier, and a handful of what appeared to be *gringos* had successfully raided his island, then ambushed, captured, and beaten his soldiers bloody (at least, that was how he heard it from the soldiers) — he was not a happy man. (Actually, it was our Panamanian buddy, Archo, who did the beating.) No, indeed, he was not a happy camper. Anyone he caught on Coiba ever again would live with the other *desperadatos* forever. *Until death did them part...*

Speaking of death and parting…

Commandant Jallente — a tallish heavyset man, nearing his fifties, with close-cropped dark hair that was suffering streaks of gray already, and almost black eyes — wasn't a bad-looking man, but he wasn't all that chipper at the best of times. He spent nearly three weeks out of four, every month, on this godforsaken island. *(Dios! He might as well be a bastardo prisionero himself!)* He had little or no ties to the mainland during those spells other than a phone that worked about half the time. And then there was his wife. Ha! *Si*, his wife… The Countess Torrana Jallente… *She was no more a countess than he was a howler monkey but she had taken to calling herself that. Merde! Most of the time she was barely his wife.*

One week every month he escaped this cursed island, only to be with a person who had married him for prestige (and two nice cars and a fairly nice condo) rather than passion. He swore she was happier when he was gone. (And so was he…almost.) But *Dios*, even at her age — a well-kept forty — Torrana was hedonic, carnal, and lustful…comfortably sliding from innocently voluptuous right into debauched. Men sensed it on her. She put off a musk — a tang of sensual possibility… *Jesus Christe! Last month he came home early and caught her with the bellboy! Merde! The bellboy! Dios!*

He hated this damned island with a passion! And that woman — she made him crazy! She was a sexual quicksand that swallowed his common sense.

He had considered leaving her. Hell, he had considered killing her, but he couldn't quite bring himself to do either. Yet…

The truth was, Commandant Martino Jallente was a man very near the end of his rope, and he was looking to punish someone for the dirty trick life had played on him. And almost anyone would do.

CHAPTER FOURTEEN

The following day we checked our gear (mostly weapons, radios, water, and a little food), then piled aboard the Goose and slipped out of Panama. We headed across a small stretch of deep-green Caribbean water and into the little sportfishing haven of Jicaron Island just a few miles west of Coiba Island. The next morning at sunrise we'd make our move to Coiba.

Into the fray, lads, into the fray, once more...

We sat around a fire at the deserted end of Jicaron that evening and went over our plans one last time. Basically, Will, Diego, and I formed the phalanx of the operation, going in after the juice...if there was any to find. Jing and her hawk, and Travis, would cover our entry and retreat. Eddie would stand at the ready for a quick exit in his Goose. It seemed pretty simple.

The first part went exactly as planned. We slipped across the eight miles of warm water to Coiba at sunrise, so close to the water you could barely call it flight. Eddie took us into the same small cove I'd used when we flew my Cessna to the island the last time. But unfortunately, although we had researched the history of the island commander, we weren't aware of the serious improvements that Commandant Jallente had made to Coiba in the last few weeks.

■ ■ ■

"There is a bogey, Commandant," said the radarman, somewhat stiff with protocol and a little discomfort. The commander had become difficult lately, hard to please and easy to anger. "We are picking up what could be a speedboat coming from the direction of Jicaron."

Normally, the personnel on the island didn't concern themselves with boats. There were almost no rescue attempts made on Coiba because once a prisoner arrived here, he or she was totally incommunicado. There was no way to find them or communicate with them in order to arrange a rescue. *Nonetheless, there were guests coming...*

"Gather a dozen men, combat-ready," said the island's commander to his operations officer. "Take the patrol boat. Move south but wait until we know where the target has landed before departing. You will communicate with our base station every quarter-hour. Understood?"

As his officer headed away on his assigned task, Commandant Jallente eased out a sigh and studied the sun rising out of the horizon like a gold doubloon, spilling a brilliant sheen across the early morning waters. For just a moment, he let his thoughts slip back to the mainland and his condo, and Torrana, his wife. He was torn between buying her the emerald ring she wanted and killing her. He still hadn't made up his mind. There were benefits on both sides of that coin. She devoured a man's common sense and could kill his pride with little more than a handful of words, but she could be so...*appreciative*...at times.

■ ■ ■

Eddie's Grumman Goose was much larger than my Cessna 182, and it was a squeeze getting it into the mangrove channel and beaching it, nose outward, for a quick departure. But we managed. Once all of us were ashore, Travis pulled out his topographical map and pinpointed one last time our points of entry and exit routes. Around us was a jungle orchestra of birds calling, monkeys screeching and hooting, and a variety of barks, calls, and an occasional growl of something bigger and unhappy with this invasion. Travis and Jing would guard the main access routes (little more than animal trails, really). Everyone double-checked their radios and weapons. Will and I carried Walther 380 PPK pistols, and I carried my newest favorite weapon, a scoped Ruger 10-22 rifle with a silencer. With subsonic (bang suppressive) hollow-point .22 caliber ammunition, it was "low-end" as far as knockdown power. But it made no more noise than a horsefly fart. You could shoot someone a half-dozen times and they'd still be trying to figure out what was happening as the lights went out.

Travis carried his riot shotgun and a bandolier of ammo. Like he said, he didn't care about sound — when he shot someone, he wanted them to stop moving right then and there.

Jing was wearing a Walther 380 pistol in a shoulder holster. Between that and her hawk, she was probably the best-armed of all of us.

Diego wasn't all that fond of guns but he chose a 9mm handgun in a side holster. It was a good, simple, all-terrain weapon.

Regardless of the weaponry, it was not our intention or our desire to shoot anyone, particularly those in any official penitentiary positions. Our hope was to dissuade anyone from bothering us with a show of force. But aside from the authorities, there were the very dangerous, completely unscrupulous *desperadatos*, and they could be an issue. In addition, we all carried the best portable satellite radios that money could buy. Fortunately, we were close enough to major cities for land-based stations and satellites to provide fair reception.

Finally, with little more than a nod and a wish of luck to each other, we were on our way. Will, Diego, and I headed into the jungle to the ruins. Travis took a trail to the east and set up a perimeter defense where the jungle thickened. Jing took the trail that ran closer to the shore, to the more open west, so she could take advantage of Cielo if necessary. .

We all recognized that at any point on this sojourn, we could be little more than a few hundred yards from one of those hellish camps. But there had been no way to get accurate locations of any of them, other than Diego's foggy estimations. We'd gotten lucky with Diego the first time we'd come through here, but like Rufus says, "*Luck is a relative thing. Sometimes you have it, mon, and sometimes your relatives have it...*"

After a last look at Travis and Jing slipping into the jungle, our friend Diego turned to Will and me. "Time to go magic juice hunting, amigos."

And so it was.

We worked our way into the interior and picked up the little creek that led toward the ruins and the strange, smooth-walled rock room that had held the bottles of vegetation elixir. As we moved along cautiously, I studied the terrain and began to notice the remains of a civilization. It was battered and buried, and hidden in the thick vines of time, but it was there. Most of it was that of an ancient Indian culture, but here and there appeared a more sophisticated relic in texture and design, and there were places where the writing changed, displaying a deeper style and intellect, and what appeared to be an entirely different language built around a more advanced grammar and structure.

Or maybe it was just what I wanted to see...

We made it to the hidden entrance in the cleft of the rock without incident, and in moments, we had opened the sliding stone door and entered the first room.

As our flashlights blushed the interior, Diego strode over to the far wall and began brushing it with his hands. Finally, he eased out a breath and the wall next to him silently slipped open about a foot.

We once again eased into the next room, our flashlights casting smoky yellow beams across the floor and walls. And still sitting peacefully against the wall was the strange, battered skeleton, and the glass-like shelf, empty, just as we had left it.

"What did you expect?" muttered Will, reading our minds. "Did you think the magic juice man was going to stop by and refill it?"

I paused for a moment and stared at the skeleton, more sure

now than before that there must have been some sort of conflict here. Maybe the people who produced the juice were escaping from the natives or the Spanish… My guess was, the folks with the magic juice would probably have been seen as gods by the natives, and that's why they left the extra bottles, thinking no one would find them, and they could come back. But they didn't. I suspected that there might have been a major disagreement of some sort. *There's nothing more aggravating than finding out your gods aren't actually gods.* And the ones who knew where the bottles were kept had escaped or had been killed…by someone.

But at best, that was a guess. And the truth was, we should have been paying more attention to the here and now rather than the then and maybe.

Only by a sheer gift of the gods did the commandant's patrol boat miss the mangrove entrance we had used to hide Eddie's plane and disembark, and this bought us some of the time we needed. But the commandant remembered where the incident with his soldiers had taken place before, so on the return trip, he had the boat unload a patrol of a dozen soldiers not a quarter-mile north of us.

Eddie was in a spot. He had determined the frequency the patrol boat was using and was monitoring them when they announced the offloading of the soldiers. He quickly contacted his team and informed us. Travis and Jing were between a rock and a hard place. They had no desire to start a shooting contest here, nor did they want to injure or kill innocent soldiers just doing their job. But they had to get Will, Diego, and me out safely. There was no way Travis would leave anyone behind.

I was studying the walls around us in the small room when our radios squelched and an unusually frantic Eddie came on, announcing the problem we were about to have. We had maybe fifteen or twenty minutes to get back or take up residence on

Coiba. Travis broke in then, saying he and Jing could hold them briefly if necessary, but we needed to get moving.

Still, through all this immediate discovery, I felt I was missing something. There had to be more than what we'd found here. There *had* to be. Why would anyone go to this much trouble to create one closet and a few bottles of plant elixir? We were missing something. Frantically, I began running my hands up and down the walls, moving from side to side, hammering the soft stone with my palms, cursing, pleading with the room to surrender its secret. I needed it. I had to have it for the sake of my son.

"Amigos, we gotta go," whispered Diego. "There is nothing here..."

I swung around, taking one last gander, and noticed something. It wasn't on the walls or the stone shelving. It was in the skeleton's clutched palm. The white finger bones were closed tightly and tucked to his side, offering almost no view of what he held. But now at this angle, I could see something — a small, metal tube maybe three or four inches long and an inch wide. At the same moment, I heard Will suck in a breath in surprise and recognition. We looked at each other but Diego was ahead of both of us. He was already moving over to the skeleton, kneeling in front of it and gently prying the shiny metal tube from the ancient soul's fingers.

Eddie could hear the voices of the men as they neared the point where his team's defense perimeters were set. So could Travis and Jing.

"Hold your positions," ordered Travis quietly into his handheld radio. "Maybe they'll move by us...and head east."

But it was wishful thinking at best.

"We're gonna have to get out of here pretty quick," I said as we knelt around the skeleton. "I don't want anything bad enough to become a resident here."

Diego straightened up and examined the plain metal tube, which was constructed of something that felt and looked like aluminum with a single button at the top. My friend looked at Will, then over to me. He held up the tube, and before I could say, "Wait!" he pressed the button.

To our surprise, nothing happened.

"Well, amigos, dat be seriously disappointing..." sighed Diego. "I mean, seriously — "

I snatched the device from Diego and pressed it again, harder, desperation overwhelming logic, and suddenly, the wall about ten feet from the "closet" where we'd found the Crazy Grow slid into itself and presented another similar shelf affair. This one had three bottles on the top. But it was obvious, by the shelving, that it was designed for much more.

I aimed at a barren wall and pressed the button again, and another closet to the right of the ones we had discovered slid open. But all the shelves were empty. There was a quick, disappointed glance between us, and I pressed the button once more, aiming in a different direction. Another stone closet opened to the far left — but again, the shelves were bare. Hugely disappointed but undaunted, I hammered the button like a teenager in a video arcade. Another wall opened behind us, but with the same disappointing results.

Again and again I pressed, my eyes beginning to carry the desperation and disappointment of a luckless Vegas gambler. No more doors opened.

"You were right," muttered Will incredulously. "I'd bet dollars to donuts this was a storage facility that could well have been built before the first primitive soul trudged his or her way across the Bering Straits and down the western coast of North America." He stared at us with a look of amazement. "But I'm guessing it might have been used later, as a storage facility for the boosting and survival of early primitive societies — select terraformation here and there. Maybe even with the Mayans and the Aztecs, or even the Incans." He eased out a breath. "But something went wrong here at some point…between the locals and the juice makers. Something that left the relatively benign visitors at odds with the community."

"Could be the visitors just offended a local god at some point," I added. "One thing I've come to realize is, religion breeds power and those who have the power don't relinquish it easily." I smiled. "It's a convenient thing, knowing what the gods are thinking and whose head they're wanting."

Diego brought us around to the here and now. "Enough talk about gods! We gotta get da hell out! Now! We gotta go!" He exhaled hard and his eyes were bright with fear and determination. "I no goin' back to dat damn prison, mons! You understand?"

That was emphasized by Eddie's voice as we heard him shouting into the radio, "Travis and Jing are taking fire! They can't hold their positions long!" There was a pause. "You're either coming or you're not…"

Without a word, we grabbed the three bottles on the shelves, threw them into a bag, and were out the door. Wisely, Diego closed all the magic closets behind us. That is to say, the openings slid magically into the rock. I could hear gunfire in the distance. Time was running out.

At that moment, Travis was playing a coy but dangerous game. He had let off an initial burst into the trees above the patrol to pin them down and buy us time. But after a few minutes of gunfire, part of the team was splitting off, trying to circle him. He could fix that easy enough but he didn't want to kill anyone if he didn't have to.

Jing was offering a short burst or two to pin down the few men coming her way, but she had the same problem. They knew where she was. The gunfire freaked out her big osprey, who had settled in the foliage above her, but Cielo boldly held his ground next to his human counterpart. There was a bond between those two that couldn't be shattered by fear or the threat of death. But there was little safety in the trees right now, and there were a lot of rounds being loosed by the spooked, battle-green soldiers.

At just about this time, Diego, Will, and I came bursting through the foliage near Jing, startling her andalmost getting ourselves shot. After a quick conference, we radioed Travis, letting him know we were safe.

Before things grew into a full-fledged firefight, the prison officer called down his men and had them hold their fire. He had decided on a pincher movement, to cut off his targets from the water and escape. The soldiers were spreading out.

Travis, who had done this more than once in much scarier places, recognized the plan. He picked up his radio and in seconds, we all knew the situation. Our big friend couldn't — *wouldn't* — let us be taken.

"You people pack up and run for Eddie and the plane, now!" he growled at his radio, staring at it as if it was a living thing. "I'm going to make a quick circle and hit them from behind. I don't plan to kill anyone if I can help it, but I'm going to draw them off of you. Don't shoot anymore if you can help it. I don't want them to know where you are."

There was a pause, then our big friend continued. His voice was gruff now — that of an officer giving orders — but I could sense the emotion. "Go! I'll keep them busy while you people get to the plane and get out of here."

"Whoa, whoa!" I shouted into my radio. "We're not leaving you behind. We're not letting you do this heroic emotional bullshit! You're coming out with us!"

There was a moment of silence, then Travis came back. "This is not emotional and it's not heroic, it's just smart. This is as close to war as you're gonna get, buddy, and war is about tough decisions. There's no goddamn point in all of us being caught or killed. I'll draw them off and give them a run for their money — get them chasing their tails." He paused. "You forget that I've done this once or twice… I got a radio, and I have weapons. I'll be fine. You get into the air and get away. Come back tomorrow and circle this end of the island late in the day, just after sunset. When I see the plane, I'll call and we'll rendezvous."

Still, I complained. I had a terrible feeling about this. But that was the plan, and while Travis made it sound like a good move, I was reminded of what Rufus occasionally said. *"De art of life be nothing more dan adjustment, mon. He who adjusts, survives..."*

I sighed and turned to Will and Diego. "Let's go. He'll figure it out. It's what he does."

Jing, sitting at the base of a big gumbo limbo tree, was listening as well. Her feathered guardian was on a branch just above her, those big yellow eyes taking in everything, every movement, every sound below. She looked up and made a motion — the circle of a finger — and in the next moment, the giant osprey spread his wings and dropped in next to her, those huge yellow eyes staring at his mistress. She reached out and drew in the hawk like a dog, her fingers grasping and ruffling his feathers affectionately. But then she spoke quietly, firmly, in a language so old that its name was lost in the circles of time. Her hand gently brushed Cielo's neck and back as the eyes of the hawk and the woman touched and held again. Then she pulled back and nodded, and the hawk, in a single sweep of its huge wings, lifted off and disappeared into the deepening shadows of the jungle.

Jing sighed. That wasn't an easy thing to do. Then she grabbed her weapon and headed for Eddie and the plane.

As Will, Diego, and I worked our way through the jungle, I could hear gunfire and shouting in Spanish, but there was nothing we could do about it right now. By the time we reached the plane, Jing was there waiting, and Eddie was doing a run-up. After stowing our precious cargo of three Crazy Grow bottles in the baggage compartment, Will got the bow rope and I got the stern, and we pulled the Goose in for boarding. We all looked at each other. In the distance, we could hear the gunfire increasing, then it stopped abruptly. The falling sun was casting twisted shadows through the mangroves and the trees.

I glanced around as we prepared to board. "Where's Cielo?"

Jing just looked at me — her eyes hard and worried at the same time. "He has business…"

I stared at her. I could see the concern, even fear. But it wasn't my call.

Eddie broke the spell. "We gotta go," he growled. "It's what he told us to do, and if anybody knows this game, it's Travis."

Five minutes later, we were in the air and headed back to Panama. It was better to seek anonymity at one of the tiny airstrips there right now. We ran out from the island right on the water so no one could easily see us and pick up the Goose's call numbers. None of the soldiers had found our plane. But there would probably be authorities looking at the islands around Coiba regardless.

We were lucky so far. We were flying away. But with Travis, it was a different matter…

CHAPTER FIFTEEN

There was no question that Travis knew the game, and for a while, he simply ran the two patrols into the ground. Then he worked his way around them, moving into the higher terrain toward the interior, leaving his pursuers exhausted and shooting at shadows. Our big friend hiked inland about a mile to where the ground began to rise, and was just starting to relax. This had gone better than he had hoped. No one would have expected him to go deeper into an island with a beastly reputation like this one. He figured he could hole up for the night and most of the next day while the soldiers at the lower end of the island chased their tails to exhaustion, then work his way back down to the shoreline for a pickup by Eddie and the Goose at sunset.

It seemed like a pretty solid plan, as far as foolishly daring plans go…

Travis was amazed at how full of life the island was — the incredible fruits and flowers, and a variety of birds and animals like nothing he had ever seen. It all seemed far too spectacular to simply be a natural progression on a little "nothing" island in the middle of nowhere. Or maybe the fact that it was in the middle of nowhere was its saving grace. But he knew that this was not paradise by any means. Twice he had hidden from groups of *desperadatos* passing along the trail he was on. They were hard-looking, shabbily dressed, bearded, and mostly barefoot, but they all carried weapons of some sort, from knives to spears.

Travis was just beginning to compliment both his skill and luck when somewhere near he smelled the smoke of cooking fires. He eased off the path for a moment and listened. He could faintly hear voices in the distance.

Curiosity is a terrible thing, especially when it's combined with a large ego. Our friend moved off the trail and onto an animal path that headed down into an enclave toward the voices, and it wasn't long before he was rewarded with the images of a tribe of *desperadatos*. There before him were crude, thatch-roofed pole huts in a jungle-cleared circle. There was a large fire pit in the center, and hanging from the branches of a couple of trees were haunches of meat and dressed birds. Here and there were the remnants of civilization — glass demijohns and metal buckets, the shards of a mirror or two lay about, and there was what looked like a rough-cut wooden latrine. It was all primitive enough to make even Travis blanch. The people that he could see — all men — were thin or wiry but not emaciated. From what Travis had observed in his recent hike, the countryside was lush with fruits and wild vegetables. You wouldn't starve here. You might not like it, but you wouldn't starve. The people were garbed in the remains of once good clothes. Some looked better than others, but no one was dressed for dinner.

As he watched, Travis noticed a large man exit one of the more acceptable huts. This guy was getting his share of the good stuff, no doubt. He was big — really tall, probably nearing six ten or eleven — and unlike most of his companions, was heavy and fairly muscled. He carried himself with a confident air and there was a certain deference paid to him.

The alpha male... While we may consider ourselves "civilized," when things get really bad we go right back to the basics of nature.

Travis was just thinking this might be a really good time to get on the road again, maybe catch a few hours' sleep and circle back to see if there were any soldiers at the pickup site that he needed to annoy. But at that moment, he heard something behind him. He was turning when he felt a stunning smack on the back of his head and the lights went out.

■ ■ ■

It was the better part of a half-hour before Travis came around. He found himself tied to a tall, heavy pole in the center of the clearing a little ways from the communal fire pit. He moved and was rewarded with a brief blast of lightning in his skull.

Around him was the *desperadato* camp. A fairly tall fellow stood off to the side, holding Travis' shotgun. (*No kindness there...)* Many of the members had taken a seat in the dirt or on logs that were close to the fire pit. There was an anticipatory feeling about the whole thing. It seemed like someone should be selling popcorn.

None of this was good. But it got worse. There in front of our companion stood the huge man he'd seen earlier. "Huge" was just an inadequate description. Up close, he was a monster, in all senses of the word. He towered above his companions, glowering and hard, the epitome of bad attitude. He was bearded but it was fairly controlled, and had jet-black hair to his shoulders. His bushy brows were furrowed but his gray eyes were bright with purpose and clever-looking. *The boss...*

Travis shook his head again, suffering the pain, trying desperately to bring himself around. The huge fellow in front of him straightened up, glanced around at the audience, then walked up to Travis and backhanded him across the face. This whole thing wasn't getting any better. It seemed he was booked as the entertainment for the evening.

"Who you be, gringo?" growled the gorilla in heavily accented English. "You be…running or watching? You be a spy, mon? From de Tatos camp? Or de prison?"

Travis was a quick study. He figured this guy thought he was a member of a competitive camp, and almost inevitably there had to be agitation between them. They were competing for survival.

"I'm not from any camp," Travis replied. "I'm from the mainland. My plane went down — crashed in the water…" *Right now, a smart lie was better than the truth.* "I'm just passing through."

"Maybe he be one o' dem from de fortress?" said a man from the gathering.

"Yes! A prisoner or a guard, huh?" barked another in Spanish.

Travis realized this wasn't going well. He was going to have to gamble. He straightened up as best he could. Being fairly fluent in Spanish (any serious soldier of fortune studied languages — it could mean the difference between life and death), he shouted, "I am what I say I am! I am not of the prison! And I challenge any man here for that truth! I claim that right as a *desperadato!"*

Diego had explained to us that, as a general rule, bloodshed was really common in this neck of the woods, and fights among *desperadatos* were generally to the death because there was nothing worse than living on an inescapable island with a conscienceless bastard who carried a grudge against you. So…

Travis shook his head again and stood tall, the sheer adrenaline of survival driving away his pain. "I will fight anyone who calls me a liar!" he cried. Then he gambled big-time. He turned to the huge leader in front of him. "Anyone! Anytime!" he shouted.

The message was deadly clear. The gauntlet had been cast. The village leader could just kill the intruder at that moment, but his power would be eroded somewhat by that. *No, he had just been challenged and he would either have to fight or walk away. It was the way of the island.*

A few moments later, Travis found himself untied and in the center of the village circle, facing the monster of a man. He knew that in a one-on-one situation, even as good as he was, he could lose. It wasn't just losing the fight, but generally, every straightforward fight could cost you — teeth, broken bones, sprains. It went with the territory. He couldn't afford that now. He had friends counting on him. But he couldn't get around this, so he had to play hard and smart.

The big guy carried a cold meanness and a confidence that came with experience. He wasn't a fool. Travis watched him glance at a companion at the side of the ring who was holding a sizable club.

(Hmmm…his insurance policy if things weren't going right…)

Travis reached into his pocket and felt around. There it was, an American quarter — change from an earlier transaction on the other side of this insanity. He took it out as the guy with the club stepped forward and shouted, "A challenge has been made! A challenge has been accepted. Let the tribe prosper from it!"

"Let the tribe prosper!" shouted the group of maybe thirty ragtag men in unison.

Travis and his opponent moved forward cautiously. Then all of a sudden, Travis stopped about four feet from his adversary and held up the coin.

"Wait! I demand a coin toss! For the first blow!" he said.

The big guy slowed his momentum, then stopped. "What da hell? You fight! Now, gringo!"

"Are you afraid of a coin toss?" shouted Travis. "For the right to the first blow?"

Well, this just thoroughly confused everyone for the moment, including the *desperadato* leader. But before anyone could make any serious decisions, Travis tossed the coin high into the air. Everyone's heads went up, eyes instinctively watching the twirling coin for a second, including the American's opponent. At that point, Travis just stepped in and hammered the fellow in the throat with a straight-armed knuckle punch.

Anyone who has spent any time studying the art of self-defense (or anyone who appreciates winning fights and keeping your teeth where they belong) will tell you there are three things to remember early on about altercations — groin, throat, and nose. A quickly executed strike or kick to any of those locations will generally suck the enthusiasm out of most opponents.

(Those of you who have been on the delivering or receiving end of these are nodding now.)

My friend struck like a snake, hammering the man's windpipe, then he stepped back, out of stumbling/clutching range. The big guy's eyes went wide and his hands instinctively went to his throat (which just wasn't working properly at the moment — a definite lack of airflow). This left the rest of his body unattended. Travis stepped in and kicked the man solidly in the groin.

The guy dropped to his knees, not sure at the moment which was more disconcerting — the agony in his groin or not being able to breathe properly. Regardless, he was out of the contest.

Travis was preoccupied at the moment and didn't notice the fellow in the crowd with the club as he stepped in and came at Travis from behind. He would have been successful and this story would have had a different ending had it not been for the feathered lightning bolt that fell out of the sky at that moment.

Cielo...

The man was charging forward, raising the club, his eyes bright with the surety of viciousness and victory, when that damned bird hit him like a freight train. For a moment or two, it was just stumbles and screams as Cielo buried his talons in the back of the man's neck and redesigned his hairline. The guy dropped the club, screaming and careening across the clearing as the hawk screeched in anger and tore at him. The circle of men broke and scattered with a good degree of terror as well. Most of them were fairly simple people. None of them had ever seen anything like this and they wanted no part of it. The truth was, they didn't dislike their leader — he was harsh but fair most of the time — but the little bastard he kept as his eyes and ears wasn't liked at all.

The show was over in a moment or two. The lackey with the club ran for the jungle, covered in blood. The hawk lifted and cried in defiance, then spun and fell again. This time, he stalled out and landed on the edge of a bamboo roof next to Travis. The message was clear.

Travis picked up the club the fellow had dropped and went over to the giant, who was still on his knees trying to recover. The American stared at the humbled man. Most of the men in that clearing knew what was going to happen. They'd seen changes of power before and it wasn't pretty. But instead of striking the prostrate leader, Travis reached down and helped the fellow to his feet. Then, of all things, he handed him the club. The eyes of the two men met and held for a moment. Travis reached out his hand, still without words, and the big man took it and smiled.

At that moment, Travis remembered an expression by a helicopter pilot-cum-guru friend of his from Vietnam — Captain Teddy Thompson, one of the fine men who lifted off one day to the thump of the rotors and never came back. *And Travis missed him.* Teddy used to say, *"All real bonds are built on faith, trust, and sacrifice, and the absolute experience of these things. Love can be a part of that equation, but in truth, it's too damned malleable and easily twisted by other emotions to be regarded as all that reliable."*

And so it was that my friend and his amazing feathered companion formed a bond, found a refuge, and spent the night at the village. Travis shared a meal and spoke with the men there, gaining insight about how the penal colony functioned and the staggered tribes across the island, possibly as many as a thousand individuals in thirty different camps. He also learned how the prison worked and about the commandant, Colonel Martino Jallente, a man who faced challenges on and off the island.

Speaking of the colonel… The man wasn't at all happy that the invaders of his island had eluded his soldiers and apparently disappeared in their plane. The soldiers saw a floatplane rise out of the water offshore and head into the darkening sky to the west. *There was no point in reporting it. By the time the lazy bastards on the mainland had pulled their heads out of their asses, the aircraft could be in Mexico.* He paused. *But his people reported gunfire and an altercation well after the plane was gone. His soldiers chased what they thought was a lone gringo. But they said he appeared and disappeared like a ghost.*

That might be worth following up… thought Jallente as he called in his second in command. "Captain Rolo, I want you to gather a six-man patrol for the interior. You leave this afternoon."

His second blanched noticeably. "For the interior, sir?"

It was a place prison personnel avoided at all costs, especially the soldiers. They were generally content to hold control over the large stone penitentiary. The only time they wanted to see the prisoners on the island was when an inmate's incarceration time was up and he appeared at the gates to be released.

"Did I stutter?" the colonel barked.

His officer flinched.

"I don't like the activity we're seeing on South Coiba," Jallente continued. "I want you to set up observation posts along the two trails that run the length of the island, about halfway down. Take enough supplies for a week, and take the patrol boat to your drop-off."

(*That was a kind bone to throw to the captain — no trekking through the jungle.*)

Jallente was in a better mood than normal. Tomorrow he had his monthly one-week rendezvous with his wife. He was leaving first thing in the morning and looking forward to some debauchery, if not a little feigned affection.

But every place of refuge has its price…

CHAPTER SIXTEEN

Speaking of refuges and prices…

As we landed at our little strip back in Panama and headed over to our motel, there was good news and bad news. The good news was, we now had three more bottles of the magic juice — probably enough to assuage the needs of the damned mafioso in Miami. But I was reminded that it really didn't matter to Travis. If he had his way, this was going to come to blows after the exchange, regardless of how many containers of juice there were.

Then, the bad news: Travis was somewhere in the jungle on Coiba and we had to find him. He had a handheld radio but there were no local towers anywhere near him, and even satellite reception was sketchy this far south.

To add to the bad news list…it just so happened that while we were preparing to head back to Panama, a whole new package of ugly was happening. Some disturbing plans for Will and I were being hatched, and there could be peripheral damage all around.

■ ■ ■

Our committed pursuers from Jamaica and the Last Resort, Quan and Tranga, had arrived in Panama and with a little investigation, had found the International Aircraft Arrival reports on Eddie's Goose and the airport of entry. They were clever folks. They'd been doing this for a while.

Once they had an airport, they simply called all the local

motels and hostels in the area until they found where we were staying. Then, after finding our motel and chatting with the receptionist, explaining to the older lady at the desk that they were old friends and that they couldn't wait to see us again, they worked up a little surprise for Will and me. Then they called a contact of theirs in the area who handled "unpleasant things that go boom." *If you live long enough, you make contacts in any business...*

They picked the lock on the motel door. Then they tied a recently purchased fragmentation grenade under the bathroom sink and ran a string to the small doorstop on the bathroom door. They were no longer considering options of negotiation or bringing us back to "Adios Island." They'd settle for a nice mention in the obits of the local paper. They could collect their money with that. The grenade in the bathroom would work just fine. Anyone who opened the door the rest of the way, or closed it, would pull the pin automatically and in about six seconds, would be on their way to Heaven or Hell. The whole thing might well be construed as a gas leak.

However, rats love to chew through string and wires. And while our Caribbean pursuers had hidden the string to the grenade fairly well, they had gone out to eat prior to their assault on us. Quan still had the rich flavor of pork rolls on his fingers, which he transferred to the cord between the grenade pin and the door. It was just too inviting for the local rat that gnawed clean through the string.

■ ■ ■

We all gathered in Eddie's room and checked the newspaper, but there was nothing regarding Coiba and the gunfight. I didn't expect anything but we had to be sure. We double-checked our gear and Eddie did a careful preflight on the Goose. We would be going back into the fray at sunset.

■ ■ ■

About that same time, Colonel Jallente was boarding a military floatplane outside the prison. It would take him to the mainland and his wife. He was a day early on his normal monthly one-week rendezvous, but he needed to make a deposit into his secret bank account — money that came from wealthy prisoners for privileges they weren't supposed to have. The colonel was hoping that Torrana wouldn't mind the surprise…

But as Rufus would tell you, *"Dere be one thing both da devil and da gods love, and dat be surprises."*

■ ■ ■

After a fairly good night's sleep in the *desperadato* village, Travis said *adios* to the giant, Papo Gacha, and his men, then prepared for his hike back toward the southern end of the island. As Papo and he shook hands, the big *desperadato* held the American's eyes for a moment and said, "Anything, anytime, amigo..."

Travis knew those words weren't spoken lightly and he appreciated it.

As he began his trek, Travis watched the hawk work its way through the canopy above with practiced ease, and he smiled. The osprey had dropped down and flared a couple of times, landing close to Travis on a branch or the ground as they paused along the trail. Travis could feel the intelligence and extraordinary insight from the creature as it cocked its big head and chirped at him in an almost human-like fashion. It left him comforted and amazed. They were getting out of this place and Travis was looking forward to a beer.

■ ■ ■

At the same time, Captain Rolo had loaded his patrol of a half-dozen men and their gear into the prison's twenty-two-foot

Aquasport. The boat pilot carried them down to the middle of the island, where Rolo and his men disembarked.

Late that afternoon, as the captain and his soldiers worked their way inshore, and Travis was moving along the trail that would take him to an estimated rendezvous point with his people, Colonel Jallente arrived at the door of his condo in Las Lajas, just west of Santiago. After depositing the latest of his ill-found wealth in his bank of choice, and armed with flowers and a honed libido, he climbed the condo stairs to the second floor, slipped a key into the lock of his apartment, and quickly opened the door. He was planning a surprise entrance, and indeed, it was…

There, tied to the living room chandelier and dangling by her wrists, was a thoroughly naked version of his loving wife. In the room with her were two men, dressed in skimpy black leather pants with open crotches and sporting Mardi Gras masks. One was holding a whip, and the other was holding himself while displaying a significant affection for Torrana Jallente's ass. (It looked like a combination of the Ringling Brothers and a Marquis de Sade act.)

The stunned colonel stood there, eyes doing a Daffy Duck bulge, mouth hanging open, flowers dangling at his side. His wife turned, as shocked as everyone else by the surprise entrance, but dealing with it fairly well. "You're home early, dear," she muttered. "You really should have called…"

Jallente was still in his military uniform and had his holstered pistol against his side. He calmly took it out.

With the first few rounds, the leather-clad duo was shrieking like monkeys as parts of the chandelier exploded in bright shards and holes began magically appearing in the terrazzo floor and the walls around them. Next, the sliding glass doors to the porch behind the two shattered and disintegrated. Torrana was trying to wrench herself loose from her bonds, having thoroughly recognized this wasn't going to end well. The two leather boys quickly decided that discretion was the better part of survival here. They were screaming and stumbling through the empty frames of the patio doors now, hurling themselves off the second-story porch with the enthusiasm of drunken lemmings.

One would have figured the sound of police sirens would have been in the wind by now, but this was Panama. The country of Panama is absolutely beautiful and the people, by and large, are wonderful. But every place of refuge, in addition to having its price, also has its crazies…and Panama has a lot of them. The police generally showed up if someone was dead, and the rule of thumb for the populace was, if it wasn't happening to you, then it wasn't happening. And of course, no one was anxious to get on the bad side of the guy who ran the dreaded Coiba Prison. So…

Señor Jallente looked up at his wife, who was still hanging from the battered, dangling chandelier, her feet nearly touching the floor now. He closed the door and slowly walked over to his faithless, pendulate spouse, who was sputtering with a little concern at this point. Jallente stared at her, then began unbuttoning his pants. "No use letting you go to waste, now that you're all warmed up."

An hour later, Colonel Jallente exited the building with a suitcase of the few things that mattered to him and stepped into a waiting cab. His wife was still…hanging around…upstairs. He was stinging with pain and damaged pride because, all things aside, he still carried an unsupported affection for the bitch. But buffered by righteousness and the image of her dangling from the chandelier as he closed the front door, he moved on. Sort of...

Colonel Jallente found himself a motel room and a bottle of good scotch, and proceeded to get seriously drunk. The following day, he returned to Coiba Island. He didn't feel much like a vacation right now.

Unfortunately, we knew nothing about this latest experience. *"All things in good time,"* somebody once said. But they probably weren't in Central America.

In the interim, Captain Rolo and his six-man patrol had been delivered to the middle-lower part of the island. Carefully avoiding the two known, smaller prisoner camps in the area, they settled into a couple of observation points along the primary jungle trail running the length of Coiba — the *desperadato highway*, as it was sometimes called.

■ ■ ■

Everything looked like it was moving along fairly well for Travis. But our normally very cautious friend realized he was just a little behind on the rendezvous with his team and he picked up his pace, heading south again, relying on Cielo to keep an eye on things. But he could have been reminded of another quote by Rufus: *"When impatience and carelessness mate, mon, the offspring is calamity."*

The real truth is, unfortunately, sometimes it just doesn't matter how careful you are. The gods just want to be entertained. And let's face it, they make the rules.

As it turned out, Cielo, the feathered guardian angel, had widened his circle around Travis, looking for a kill for himself. And in those few minutes, Travis just happened to walk right into the colonel's largest patrol, which had spread out across the trail while they waited for two of the team to return from a scout. It was just bad timing. Before Travis realized it, soldiers appeared from both sides of the jungle, weapons at the ready. Any attempt at resistance was suicide.

Our big friend eased out a sigh and dropped his weapon, and a half-hour later he was trussed up and headed out of the jungle toward the waiting Aquasport at the water's edge. The team had been dogged continually by a huge osprey during their exit. They all took a few shots at the bird, which were apparently unsuccessful, and it disappeared.

Colonel Jallente was pleased with the capture of the gringo. It did indeed lift him out of his cuckolded funk a little. (*He had always known that his woman was somewhat sexually unwrapped, he just hadn't experienced this level close up.*)

Jallente was so taken by the capture, he ran a background check, then contacted his superiors on the mainland and informed them. They too were somewhat pleased, and a little concerned with what exactly a highly decorated American veteran was doing on their island. They assumed it probably had to do with a possible prison break. The military and civil authorities tightened things down a little, but they couldn't help giving the information to the newspaper agencies. It might help them identify the intent of the man, and identify his companions, if there were others.

By luck more than planning, we caught the news about the capture of an American on Coiba Island. There was no identification on him yet — or at least the authorities weren't releasing any at this point. But for us, there was no question as to who it was. This was not good. And Travis was evidently being held at the island fortress prison for now, and that was not good either. But at least we knew where to look.

Will, who had done the background research on this mission, including individuals we might have to deal with, was somewhat familiar with Colonel Jallente. While we sat around the motel room trying to figure out how to save our friend and get the hell out of Panama with the magic juice, Will sat up suddenly.

"You know, when I was researching this place, this colonel fellow was mentioned a couple of times. The article said he spent three weeks a month there on Coiba, and generally only one week a month on the mainland…with his wife." Will glanced around at all of us and exhaled heavily. "I'm not at all excited about getting into the people-snatching business, but maybe, just maybe, we could steal something he wants…and quietly make a trade."

"You know what you're saying here," Jing cautioned, a finger in the air. "You're talking about kidnapping."

Will shrugged, wobbling a hand. "Eeaahhh, sort of. I mean

really, we don't want to keep or hurt anything he owns. We just want to make a trade."

"Do you know what would happen to us if we got caught by de authorities doing this?" Diego muttered. "We never see de light of day again, amigo…"

Eddie took a look around the room. "I got a question for all of you. Who here can say that the fact that you're sitting here right now, alive and well, has nothing to do with Captain Travis Christian?" He waited. "Go ahead, raise your hand."

There was a subdued, almost guilty silence. There wasn't a soul in the room who wasn't beholden to that man for the air they were breathing at that moment. Travis had saved our collective and individual asses so many times, there was just nothing left to argue.

Will exhaled hard and looked around at us. "Okay," he said. "How do we do this thing?"

After a little discussion, we decided the best approach would be to check out the wife first, find out what we were up against — housing security, neighbors, access in and out, and personality. We could only hope that she was a reasonably sensible person.

Right... When elephants fly and hummingbirds dance on the heads of tigers...

Ironically enough, Jing found a small piece in the newspaper the following day regarding some sort of altercation at the residence of the officer in charge of the Coiba Island Penal Camp and Prison. (*She was trying not to show it, but she was worried for her winged companion.)* The Las Lajas police described it kindly as an altercation involving two "associates" of the wife. We needed an in here, and we needed to move quickly, before the colonel or the Panamanian government did something ugly and made all this, including Travis, disappear.

We decided to send in either me or Diego, disguised as a condominium repair and design specialist because apparently, the article indicated that the woman's condo needed some restoration. Diego had the looks and we both spoke the language, but admittedly, without ego, I was known as the smoothest talker of our team.

I wasn't the least bit hot on this idea, but neither was Diego. It was about then that I remembered the coin that my old friend Rufus had given me — the one that always came up tails.

I held up a hand. "Wait, let's just flip a coin on this. Winner stays, loser goes." I looked at my Panamanian buddy.

He paused for a moment, then shrugged. "Okay."

I reached into my pocket and found the strange coin. (It felt oddly warm…) I looked at Diego again and showed it to him. At a distance, it didn't look that different from any other old coin. "You heads, me tails, okay?"

Again, Diego shrugged. "Fine…"

I tossed the coin high into the air and let it fall onto the tiles, still nowhere certain that this was going to work, but it was better than nothing. The money piece clattered across the floor, spun dramatically, and collapsed — tails up.

I had to smile. It appeared Rufus had come through again.

Five minutes later, we got the address for the condo from the article in the paper, then had a handful of business cards made at a one-hour printer downtown. Diego's mission was pretty simple — could Torrana Jallente be turned into an asset? Or, if at all possible, could she be used as a trade for our friend?

■ ■ ■

When Diego (the condo repair specialist) arrived at the colonel's residence, he discovered it was definitely in need of some renovation. There had either been a seriously wild party or an earthquake with gunfire. While Diego did a walkthrough, Torrana Jallente followed him like a hungry puppy.

Somehow, very carefully, Diego turned the conversation toward Torrana's husband and what had happened. The woman was more than willing to verbally eviscerate Señor Jallente —

"de caveman bastard" — who had no understanding of her loneliness and her…needs.

Diego wanted to remind her that her habit of apple-bobbing every other guy she bumped into diminished the emotional authenticity here but he kept quiet and nodded. He saw an opportunity to play his hand.

"It is too bad, what he did to you — a woman who simply possesses too much love…" Diego commiserated. "I am sorry. But I must be honest with you now. I too have suffered at the hands of this man. He holds my brother in his island prison." Diego sighed sadly. "I am so sorry. I must admit I came to you today to use you, to help my brother, who is in the island hellhole your husband oversees." He shrugged and was silent for a few seconds. "But I see you have suffered much too at the hands of this same man. You, an innocent woman, whose only crime is loneliness and…occasional passion." Once again he sighed, then asked quietly, "People who hurt people should pay a price, don't you think?" He paused. "Would you like to return some of this pain? Make him pay a little? For the shame? And the hurt?" He shrugged. "I think he deserves it."

Torrana exhaled thoughtfully. "Perhaps…perhaps I should." She straightened up. "After all, I am the victim here… Did you know he brings hookers into Coiba Prison once a month for his soldiers and himself?"

Diego offered a commiserative sigh and began to explain the story of the loss of his brother, who was in Coiba Prison now for nothing more than mistaken identity, and how it had occurred to him that if Torrana would help his family, he might be able to free him. He admitted that he felt ashamed to have attempted to use her…

Torrana Jallente cocked her head and stared at Diego, a new light in her eyes. "Tell me more of this plan…"

Diego took her to the couch and explained an idea he had recently come up with after meeting her and learning more about this horrible man to whom she was married.

What if they were to pretend that she had been taken prisoner by Diego? Then they could work out a trade — her for Diego's half-brother — an American who was simply exploring the island of Coiba when he was captured. What if they were to say that Torrana would be harmed if Colonel Jallente didn't release the innocent young man?

She smiled. "Hmmmm… Okay, I like this," she said sensually. She slid over next to Diego and purred like a horny cat. She put her arm around his neck. "I like this plan. We should…discuss it more… Now, do you have somewhere you have to be at this moment, or for the afternoon?"

Diego returned to us somewhat disheveled and limping, with his eyes slightly glazed. He held up his hand and shook his index finger. "Dat woman is scary… We got to get dis done quick — I can no do that again. There are parts of me that need time to heal…"

CHAPTER SEVENTEEN

The plan was fairly simple. Diego would call the prison, get the colonel on the line, and tell him that he and his friends had kidnapped his wife. Then we'd begin negotiations for an exchange.

The only real fly in the ointment was Colonel Jallente's growing disconnection to his woman. Somewhere along the line (probably culminating when he walked into his condo and saw his wife in a *ménage à trois* with the black leather boys), the colonel's appreciation for his relationship with Torrana had slipped a little. He wasn't without affection for her, unfortunately, but there was a fairly strong desire to get even...with somebody. And almost anyone would do.

The phone in the colonel's prison office rang. "Colonel Jallente here."

"Hello, Colonel," Diego said firmly. "I'm calling to let you know that we, the People For Peaceful Island Environments, have taken your wife hostage. Let it be clear that we are demanding the release of a prisoner you have recently detained on Coiba Island. A man who has done nothing — an innocent naturalist trapped on your island and taken by your soldiers."

"The fellow had a rifle, a pistol, a radio, and some kind of hawk with him," said the colonel, not too ruffled. "And I suspect he was involved in a jungle altercation the night before with my men..." He paused. "And I don't think this gringo is a naturalist."

"It doesn't matter what you think he was or is," Diego replied with a degree of confidence. "If you want your wife back...healthy...you will leave our associate at a location of our choosing."

"Or what?" asked the colonel calmly.

Diego pulled the phone from his ear and looked at it, then he glanced at us. Will and I shrugged. Diego ad-libbed. "Or we will kill her!" he cried.

"Do you promise?" said Jallente.

"What?"

"Do you promise to kill her if I fail to comply?"

"Of course! Of course!" cried Diego, a little flustered now. "We are terrible people! We will rape her and kill her!"

"Good, good! I like the raping part," said Jallente, showing some enthusiasm for the first time. "Although she may well enjoy that too much." He paused. "Be careful," he added. "She bites like a rabid ferret when aroused."

Diego stared at the phone again, then looked over at us, his eyes wide with helplessness. Then he returned to the commander and the phone again. "Sir, we are talking about punishing your wife here," he said, losing a little of his kidnapper demeanor.

"Yes, indeed," muttered Jallente. "And I'm talking about that woman screwing half the pizza delivery boys in Las Lajas while I'm stuck in this godforsaken jungle island three weeks out of every four. I'm talking about coming home and finding her tied naked to a chandelier while she's being *jingoed* by masked men in crotchless tights! Perhaps you can imagine how that sort of thing can begin to tarnish a relationship, eh?"

Diego paused and asked quietly, "Do you not love her anymore?"

There was a pregnant pause because, damn all that was honest, the colonel couldn't quite get past his feelings for the woman. But he still wanted someone to pay, and these people were available for a dose of wrath. *Yes, they and their soldier/naturalist would do just fine...* And in truth, there was something about the man he had captured — the big gringo... There was a thing about the fellow's demeanor. He was serious military of some sort, not some simple flower-picking naturalist.

Jallente smelled something off here...

"And in truth, I have heard rumors of the hookers from Santa Catalina, who are boated into the Coiba Island fortress one Saturday every month for personnel morale…" Diego continued, sensing the mental turn and moving to the attack.

That took the colonel aback. He didn't think too many people knew about the occasional "morale-boosting" activities for personnel at the prison. But, he figured, if this man knew, his wife probably knew, and she obviously hadn't particularly punished him for shlonging a couple of hookers on occasion. Jallente paused and blinked. *Hmmmm...*

Diego continued. "Your wife is an understanding woman, eh? And what is good for the goose is good for the gander, eh?" There was a pause. "Now really, Colonel, wouldn't you like your woman back? We can make a simple trade. The gringo for your wife."

There are a lot of ways to play this, the colonel thought. If he did it right, he could get his wife and the gringo…and the asshole on the phone.

"Okay, okay, señor," said Jallente. "We will make a trade. Do you wish to come to the fortress?"

Diego huffed. "Ooohh no, I don' think so. We want to walk away from the meeting."

"Where then?" replied the colonel. "If I were you, I would begin with some haste here because your friend is not a registered, official prisoner and he could…*disappear*…at any time without a trace. C*omprende?"*

Diego had been a Coiba island prisoner, a *desperadato,* for a year. He knew that island well. "There is a lagoon and a small horseshoe beach about seventy-five yards wide right at the southern end of the island," he replied. "It is a quarter-mile south of where your men came in the other night. I am sure your missions officer knows the location. We will meet you there just before sunset. Just you and a few of your soldiers. Do you understand? This is not a fight. It is just an exchange. We simply want to give you your wife and receive our friend."

"Of course," replied the colonel. "You have my word." (Which wasn't generally worth a hot squat — but strangely enough, Jallente found he did want the woman back...) Possession, for some people, is nine-tenths of affection.

■ ■ ■

Meanwhile, back at the Rancho Bueno Motel, Quan and Tranga had again picked the lock on room 16 and entered. They had to find out why there had been no explosion. They had carefully moved to the bathroom and slowly slid the door open when they realized there seemed to be a connection problem with the grenade. Tranga bent down and found the severed string. She was holding it when a rat appeared out of nowhere. *(Probably the same one who had worked on the string earlier, and was coming back for seconds.)*

Quan was okay with the rodent's sudden appearance. They had lived in Vietnam as children — they'd seen rats. But Tranga still carried a…*thing*…about the nasty little creatures.

"Chit! Iiiieeee! Rats! Chit! Chit!" she yelled out and instinctively jerked up and away. But…she was still holding the string to the grenade pin. There was a distinct snap. She looked down at the pin dangling on the string in her hand, then up to her brother, and their eyes got that Wile E. Coyote look (*as he steps off the proverbial cliff*). "Chit…" she muttered.

In the next second, they were clawing their way out of the bathroom. They had six seconds (pretty much standard timing on grenade detonation). But the screeching and stumbling and clutching at each other as they struggled out of the bathroom and across the motel room took them seven.

Not good…

"Chit..."

Afterward, the room looked like a hurricane had hit it and they looked like refugees from an Alice Cooper concert and three-alarm fire — frizzed, smoking hair, fried eyebrows, clothes tattered, and enough lacerations to look like they'd been contestants in a bobcat enema contest. But the bathroom had taken the brunt of the explosion and they were alive, and there was something to be said for that.

The two money-collecting hit people were still in the local emergency room getting a few things patched as the sun neared the horizon and Crazy Eddie banked his big bird, at Diego's guidance, dropping her into the small lagoon in front of an almost picturesque little beach. Jing, Diego, and I, along with the colonel's wife, took the inflatable dinghy to shore while Eddie stayed at the controls of the plane. Will tossed out the small breakaway anchor on the Goose, then crouched by the hatch with a rifle.

As we slid the inflatable onto the beach and got out, there stood the colonel, at the edge of the jungle, in the shade of a trio of coconut palms with two soldiers. I was surprised at Jallente's lack of support. What I couldn't have known about were the other half-dozen well-armed men he'd sent in by boat a couple of hours earlier. They were spread out in a semi-circle around him along the shore, just inside the jungle. They had been ordered to watch their officer. When he raised his arm, or if negotiations suddenly went south, they were to "present themselves with force." Jallente would have preferred that this didn't end up in a firefight. But when it came to him or someone else getting the short end of the stick, it was always going to be someone else. And it seemed lately he didn't care so much about peripheral damage.

About that time, as I stood on the beach, I thought I heard a hawk call out in the distance. But there was no sign of one in the sky. I listened, then glanced over at Jing. She too had her head cocked, listening, her eyes searching the horizon. But there was nothing.

As the colonel watched us from the sandy strip of beach by the water, he casually flicked the receiver on his vest radio.

"Everyone stand ready," he whispered harshly. "No one acts until my command, when I raise my hand. But do not shoot my wife! Understand? My men and I will detain the big gringo. Try not to kill his companions if possible… But do what you have to, to control this."

We had underestimated the colonel's temperament, which had really gone south, and he wanted someone to pay for it. *(Never underestimate a woman's ability to forge a man's disposition…)*

Jallente waited impatiently as Jing, Diego, Torrana, and I approached him. All this had taken a few minutes, and in the process, the colonel was certain he heard the shuffling of someone in the green darkness of jungle behind him.

"Stay quiet, imbeciles!" he hissed into his shoulder mike. "Don't move until my command!"

At the same time, a shadow darted over the hot sand behind them. But it was lost as a cloud buried the glare of the brilliant sun.

Slowly, we moved across the yellow beach to the filtered shade of the palms. When we stopped, I took Torrana's arm and brought her forward.

"Here is your woman, as promised," I said. "Now, where is our friend?"

The colonel drew himself up and shrugged, the hint of an ugly smile touching his lips. "Your friend has made my life difficult on a couple of occasions," he growled in English. "I think maybe we keep him for a while." He raised a finger, confident now. "In fact, I think maybe we keep you too. And one move from the gringo on the flying boat and we will sink him!" Suddenly, he turned and shouted confidently, "Soldiers, forward!"

But nothing happened. It was really quiet.

"Soldiers, forward! Now!" cried the colonel again, his voice touching a slightly higher octave. "Soldiers…" he muttered, the last of his bravado definitely sliding into concern.

Then, from the greenery behind Jallente, the big elephant ear plants parted here and there and out came his soldiers…meek, unarmed, and very unhappy. A couple of them were displaying fresh bruises. But that was the least of the surprise. Behind them came Travis, untied and healthy, and as the verdant tropical green behind him separated once more, it revealed a huge man with long black hair, bushy eyebrows, and smart gray eyes. It was Papo Gacha, the huge boss of the inland *desperadatos* tribe who Travis had fought, then spared earlier in this adventure. Papo had seen this coming and decided to repay a favor.

The eyes of the two big men met. "We are even now, gringo…" said Gacha in that heavy voice.

Travis offered one of his rare, absolutely genuine smiles. "Oh man, we are so even…"

Then Gacha faced the colonel. "We wish you no harm, señor," said the *desperadato*. "But this man is a friend of mine." He turned to us and motioned with his head toward the waiting plane. "You should go, while you can."

"But these men…" I said, glancing at the seriously frightened soldiers, a little concerned with the outcome here.

"They will be freed," Gacha said again. "We need no more challenges than we already have."

"They won't come after you?" I asked hesitantly.

The fellow smiled but it wasn't pretty. "The jungle belongs to us and they know it. In the dark green, we are mist and smoke...and we leave scars."

About that time, I heard Cielo call out, and there he was, soaring out of the clouds like a feathered watchdog. Jing looked up and smiled with relief. She called to him with words that came from eons ago. The hawk answered and circled tightly above us. Jing quickly slipped on her leather gauntlet to protect her forearm from the crushing power of Cielo's talons. The bird watched from the sky with absolute understanding, then dropped the moment she was done, flaring perfectly and grasping her arm as gently as possible.

Travis exhaled and gifted us with another of his rare smiles. "It's time to go, my friends," he said. "We have other places to be."

As we trudged away through the hot yellow sand, Papo Gacha and his people slid into the jungle shadows and were gone.

Colonel Jallente exhaled heavily and shrugged as we waded out to the dinghy. *(You win some, you lose some...)* Then he stepped over to his wife. He reached down and took her hand. "C'mon, Chiquita," he whispered, his eyes glancing around, then softening just slightly. "This is no place for a woman as passionate as you."

And Señorita Jallente was quite taken by the compliment.

CHAPTER EIGHTEEN

At sunrise the following morning, we were in the air and headed home. It had been another remarkable adventure, to say the least. There would be a few people who would remember us, and very few who would talk about the occasion. That was generally the way it was with adventurers and seekers of fortune. Their stories were best told with beer and tequila and friends in the corners of smoky bars. I came away convinced that, aside from the exploit itself, there was nothing more mind-expanding than the experience of other people and places. Once again, I was reminded that of all the books in the world, the best stories are found between the pages of a passport.

(Those of you who have been there and done that are nodding your heads and smiling right now...)

Tranga and Quan were also on their way out of Panama, limping off into the sunset, considerably more bandaged than they were when they came in. They were a vision of injured animosity. But they knew where we were headed and they had plans.

■ ■ ■

The trip back to Key West was uneventful, thank God. We'd had enough adventure for the moment. But after hastily unloading, cleaning, and storing gear, we were all well aware that there was still another chapter to write here. We'd made our deadline and pulled off this last remarkable gig in six days, but now we had a meeting in Miami. It was time to get Tax back by surrendering the last three bottles of extraterrestrial Crazy Grow.

There was no question about what we had to do because there was nothing more valuable than a member of our crew (who just happened to be my son). But it cut to the core of all of us that we were being used, manipulated, by some mafioso asshole. Of course, Travis already had plans regarding this — no one stole from Travis, and no one threatened any of his people. But first things first…

As soon as I got home, I called the chemist at Organic Analysis Incorporated in Miami. Ten minutes later, we got a call from the big mafioso guy we'd met a week earlier. There was no greeting, no small talk.

"So, what do you have for me?" he said.

I exhaled. "We discovered three more bottles in another part of the cave system, but that was it, that was absolutely all there was. We checked every inch of the…facility…"

"If you're holding out on me —"

"What's the point?" I interrupted harshly. "What the hell would be the point? Do you really think I'm going to freaking cheat you at this while you hold my son?"

I think the anger and frustration in my voice rang true enough to back him off. There was a pause, then he came back. "Okay, amigo, this is what you do. You get your ass up here to the office with the three bottles, tomorrow, noontime, and we'll make an exchange." There was another pause. "If you're lying to me, if I find out you tried to cheat me…I'll—"

I guess I'd just had all I could handle of people wanting to hurt or cheat me and the people I cared about. "For God's sake! You freaking asshole!" I cried, shaking the phone in front of me and shouting into it. "We're talking about my son here! I don't give a rat's ass what kind of conscienceless piece of shit you are. But that's my boy you have, and there isn't enough magic juice or American dollars in the goddamned world for me to take a chance on his survival! Do you understand?"

There was a definite pause, then the guy replied with most of the bravado in his voice notched down a level. "Okay, mister, okay. Tomorrow, noon, here at the facility. Bring it all and you get the kid."

An hour later, the team was gathered again in the back room of Eddie's bar. No rest for the weary and the wicked, they say… But this wasn't just a mission. They had taken one of our people and with Travis, that was a cardinal, pretty much fatal sin.

After a brief discussion, Travis stressed that the most important, primary objective was getting Tax back without retaliation if at all possible. But this required some finesse. The problem for us lay in being able to eliminate the key players — the mafioso and maybe his two lieutenants. But first, we had to make sure our boy was safe and in our hands, and that meant giving them what they wanted. But like our big friend said, that didn't mean we had to let them keep it.

"We don't have to fight the whole mafia organization. We just have to get rid of the ones bothering us," Travis explained as he glanced around at all of us. "I don't want to do a gunfight in the middle of Miami if we can help it. The South Florida authorities would never be our friends again." He exhaled heavily. "But I've got an idea. I have to make a phone call and call in a big favor…"

And indeed, it was a hell of an idea. Certainly one of those barroom tales that no one would believe.

Travis took a sip of his beer and turned to Eddie. "I heard you brag once about having an ounce of real curare taken from that village of jungle women you 'stayed with' for a while last year. Is that true? Do you really have some curare?"

Eddie nodded. "Damn straight, amigo. I sure do. I tested it on some rats a while back, and on a damn cat that was killing the tropical birds in my backyard. It's a little old but it works like a freaking charm. If you don't use too much on your target, they can't move a muscle but their eyes are still blinking. And they're that way for the better part of a day." He paused. "But you use too much, and they don't move anymore, at all…"

Travis nodded, obviously pleased. "Make sure that's handy. We're going to need a little for the darts..."

Darts? I looked at Will. His eyebrows bounced and he shrugged.

Our leader turned to me then. "You, me, and Cody will be the pickup team in the chemical company office. Our job will be to make the exchange for Tax. We'll be armed with pistols of choice." He held up a finger. "But, for the time being, I need you and Will to find me three pellet guns and the dart projectiles that can be used with them, okay?" He wagged his finger. "Darts, not pellets, and I want *smallish* CO_2 handguns if possible." He paused, as if coming to a decision, and turned to Will. "I've heard you two talk about using pellet guns before — for fun and to solve small problems. Are you good enough to hit someone at say, inside of fifty feet?"

"Hell yes," replied Will without hesitation. "I can shoot the balls off a frog at that distance." He grinned. "If he squats and holds his ass up a bit."

"What about you, Diego?" Travis continued. "Can you use a pellet gun without any issues?"

"*Si,* amigo, *si,*" our Central American friend replied. "No *problemo*."

Travis looked at Jing. "What about you?"

"On a bad day, I can keep a four-inch grouping at thirty feet," she replied, deadpan.

Our big friend smiled and nodded. He wasn't surprised. "Okay, that's what I wanted to hear." He stood. "Wait, there's one other thing. Who knows a tattoo artist with a bad memory that we can borrow for a day or two? Someone who can keep his mouth shut."

There was a pause, then Eddie came back, "Yeah, I know someone. Good dude, ex-military — 101st Airborne."

Travis nodded. "Okay. You can tell him up front that the guys who get this tattoo aren't gonna like it." He paused. "But it probably isn't gonna matter."

There was a kettledrum sound to that statement. No one asked the obvious question.

Our friend continued. "You folks find the things we need and we'll meet back here in a couple of hours." He sighed, a little on the heavy side. "Now, Eddie, if you'll let me use your office, I have a call to make."

Once again we were about to embark on another wild-haired mission — the kind of stupid shit that would give Arnold Schwarzenegger hives. But hell, if you're not willing to challenge the extraordinary, then you have to settle for the ordinary. And no one at the bar will listen to your stories.

■ ■ ■

Travis sat at Eddie's incredibly messy desk and pulled a number out of his wallet. It was a number he hadn't used in a long time — a friend of his who had been at the short end of an ugly situation in a miserable jungle in Southeast Asia a few years back. But some things you just don't forget. And Travis was counting on that. There was also the fact that our military was in the middle of another situation right now, running down Saddam Hussein in Operation Desert Storm (which actually fit well into his plans). "Could I speak to Colonel Robertson, please," he said.

"I'm sorry, sir, the colonel is in a staff meeting right now," said a polite but firm voice. "Can I have him call you back?"

"Tell him it's Travis Christian, if you would, please."

A moment later, the colonel was on the phone.

"Long time, old friend," said the gravelly voice, and it carried deference rarely heard from a commanding officer.

But there was a time when Robertson wasn't a commanding officer, just a jackleg lieutenant two weeks fresh off a C-141 at the Da Nang Air Base and trapped in the jungle in a firefight with Vietnam regulars who knew what the hell they were doing. He had radioed his position and begged for help but nothing good happened. This was part of a sudden North Vietnam push, and several units were in the middle of hell. He had three men left that weren't dead or wounded and he was scribbling out a few final words to his wife before he died, when out of the sky, like some sort goddamned avenging angel, came this helicopter. He knew the pilot had to be crazy (and he was), but the fellow had a gunner on the fifty-caliber at the open door, and that annoyed the enemy just enough for a two-minute landing and takeoff in a place that left maybe a foot of leeway between the jungle and the rotors.

After a few moments of "catch-up," Travis came to the point and explained that he needed a favor. He wanted to borrow a small personnel transport vehicle for a couple of hours, and three or four regular military uniforms — large and medium.

That in itself didn't sound so impossible, but there was a second part to the request that stretched things a little. While they did have fairly regular flights to a couple of military bases in the Middle East (given the present situation happening with Desert Storm), it would still require some serious string-pulling.

There was silence on the phone for a moment. This was the kind of thing that could cost a man his career if it went sideways, and Travis wondered if time and position had sanded off the edges of memory. But they hadn't.

"When and where," said the colonel.

You see, Colonel Robertson remembered what had happened long ago, but he also remembered why…

When all was said and done that day, and they were back at Da Nang having a beer, the young officer, who would later become a notable colonel, stared at the helicopter pilot across the table and asked, "Why? Why did you do what you did for me and my men today? There was no percentage in it. We should both be dead now — me because of stupidity and bad luck, and you because of some sort of misplaced sense of ego or duty or whatever the hell it was."

The answer Travis had provided was something the man would never forget. Travis stared back at him. "Because I felt like it was a hill worth dying on."

A hill worth dying on. It was an expression that Lieutenant David Robertson never forgot. *A hill worth dying on...*

The young officer was reminded by that man and those words that there were those who had witnessed firsthand gallantry and death, and when they spoke of sacrifice, they understood it. These were the souls who had seen the misery born from the promises of equality and comfort without effort, the failure to practice the elements that bind us as a nation — compassion, sacrifice, and love of country — and the resulting collapse of societies that failed the test. Travis understood that there were hills worth dying on, and the amalgam of those times changed a country, maybe even the world.

Sometimes just a few words can shout across the canyons of human intellect and ideals. And there are those who have the tenacity, the internal fortitude, to decide that this place, this hill, is worth dying on — not for yourself, not for any selfish images of post-mortem recognition or glory, but for those who would come behind.

Yes, the colonel never forgot those words.

■ ■ ■

Speaking of challenging missions...

Our myopic, pretty much unsuccessful bounty hunters from the Last Resort had just landed in Key West, having ferreted out our direction of flight from the Panama FOB with a fifty-dollar bill. They headed into town from the airport, got a room at a local hostel, and unloaded their scant gear. Quan remembered one of us mentioning a place called "Crazy Eddie's Bar and Swill." Like Tranga said, they didn't get paid on these gigs without collecting the money owed by the target or an obituary, and when it came to the two gringos, they were leaning toward the obituary.

As things sometimes seemed to happen with my partner and

me (most people call them coincidences, but as Rufus has often proclaimed, it's just the gods moving the pieces on the chessboard of life), ill timing and strange luck were about to strike again.

Quan and Tranga were about to experience a gift from the gods. They were having a bite to eat at a little streetside Asian vendor when they saw Will and me park at a local sports store off North Roosevelt Boulevard (looking to get our air guns and darts). They followed us back to Crazy Eddie's. Now they had us both. But they had to be subtle. They didn't have any more grenades, and no real weapons, so they decided to be particularly clever (which had never been one of their strong points).

It so happened that Quan knew a guy who lived in Key West, and on occasion, would help people make other people have "accidents." The guy, Bobby Bingo, wasn't really much of a player in the world of revenge, and he made sure he was never around when whatever was going to happen, happened. Basically, he was a spooky little guy with a partial lisp, but he did have a particular niche in the world of bad. He specialized in things that bite and sting — poisonous snakes, black widows, scorpions, and occasional items that might be rabid. That always scared the shit out of people, and he sold these things to the folks who had issues with other folks. He would tell you it was amazing how many angry souls were wandering around the Florida Keys.

This week he had a special on Central American black scorpions, which he said were considered quite deadly. Supposedly, one good sting from that curvaceous barbed tail and you had about ten minutes before you were at the doors of Heaven (or hell, for most of his customers). He also had a special on rabid rats. (He really wasn't sure they were rabid, but they were mean little bastards that would bite just about anything that got close to them, which made them popular sellers.)

However, there was one small catch and that was the fellow's integrity. He ran out of killer black scorpions early in his sale, so he took a handful of regular scorpions (which would still sting the crap out of you, but generally wouldn't kill a person), and gave them a quick shot of black spray paint. Now there were a couple of things here to deal with: First off, the paint blocked their pores to the point that they could possibly die, but until then, they were some really pissed-off creatures.

So it was that Tranga and Quan purchased a half-dozen "killer scorpions," which they now had in a jar with a tightly sealed lid, and, just to cap the plan, they threw in a few possibly rabid rats, which were loosely contained in a small shoebox.

The Twins were going all out. The plan was to break into the homes of their two targets and slip the deadly little creatures into their beds. They were tired of this strangely unsuccessful game and were ready to check out and head back to the real islands. Like Tranga said, "We find dem assholes, get dem stung and bit, and watch da obits for da next day. Den we go home."

So, with a loosely bound shoebox of rabid rats and a jar chock-full of what they thought were deadly black scorpions, they set out to find my unsuspecting friend and me.

Aahhh, and this is where those damned bored gods stepped in...

The Twins were moving along comfortably, headed out to Stock Island and Will's boat as their first stop. They were sliding through the intersection at Sigsbee Road in Key West when suddenly, a handful of hippies in a battered Chevy van ran the red light and slammed smack dab into them.

This was not a good thing, certainly, but no one was seriously injured in the hippie van. They were too high to feel pain anyway. The problems were in the Jamaican collectors' smallish rental vehicle. At the moment of collision, the jar between the seats rocketed into the dash and exploded in a shower of glass and arachnids. Scorpions everywhere, and not just regular scorpions, but seriously agitated, purely claw-snapping, mandible-mashing crazy little bastards. (Even if they were spray painted, or maybe *because* they were spray painted.)

The shoebox, which had been put in the back seat window (as far away as possible from the occupants), went flying forward like a rat bomb. It hit the front window above the dash and burst open like a surprise package from hell. *Bam!* There were rabid rats everywhere in the blink of an eye, squealing, scampering across the dash, down into the seats, and onto the floor, joining forces with the already incensed scorpions. Quan and Tranga, at this point, had also joined in the melee. The scorpions were equally unhappy but less vocal about the whole thing.

Somehow, before our dazed hitters could pull themselves together, one of the scorpions with a poor sense of direction ended up crawling up Quan's pant leg. When dizzy Quan came around, the first thing he noticed was how his crotch was moving. Instinct, terror, and stupidity took over and he struck at the intruder. But one of the first rules in life for men is, *never hit yourself in the groin.* Quan was instantly reminded of this, but it got worse.

The man's strike immediately pissed-off the scorpion, which had just recognized what looked like the head of a one-eyed rat next to it — one of its arch-enemies in life.

(Yes, it was a head, of sorts, but not that of a rat.)

In immediate self-defense, the scorpion latched onto the one-eyed creature and struck with its curved, poison-darted tail. It was only a glancing blow, with a minimal amount of poison delivered because there was a lot of movement going on at the time, but Quan didn't know this. He was in the process of ripping down his pants and trying to remove the clawed creature, crawling/stumbling from the car and screaming incoherently, when the airbags (delayed by some sort of malfunction…or by the gods, who were really enjoying themselves) finally activated.

After the ensuing airbag explosion (which sent our nemesis flying out of the door like Superboy on crack), Quan found himself lying there, a half-dozen feet from the car, staring up at the sun, pants down, genitals fully exposed to God, country, and the immediate audience (which included people in stopped cars and thoroughly entertained pedestrians around the intersection) with a rat on his chest.

And then there was Tranga who, unbeknownst to most with maybe the exception of her brother, had just recently had breast implant surgery. She had always possessed rather small breasts and had decided to fix this in a fairly serious fashion just a few weeks ago. (She had been somewhat hesitant to take on this job, given the circumstances, but it was going to be such an easy thing. Just collect a handful of dollars from two stupid *Americanos* who didn't pay their bill at the Last Resort. What could go wrong?)

Well, what went wrong right now was the airbag on her side, which had burst from the glove compartment on impact and exploded outward like the devil's own hemorrhoid. The damned thing smacked her squarely in her new braless breasts — right where she'd just had the new jell-filled implants that were now taking on entirely new dimensions and locations from the impact.

Tranga screamed and threw up her hands, pinned to the seat, hissing curses that would whither a trucker, until a guy in the gathering crowd stepped over, pulled a Buck knife from his hip, and stabbed the airbag. There was another explosion, which did nothing good for our Asian huntress and her new boobs.

By the time the police arrived and Tranga had been removed from the car, her new silicone transplants had seriously relocated. The new design had her nipples looking like they were trying to find something under her armpits. On the other side of the car, she could just hear her brother hissing hateful curses about rats and scorpions, and crazy damned Americans.

It was well into the late afternoon before the two Jamaican collectors of money or souls were released from the emergency room. Both had required a few stitches here and there, again… as well as tetanus shots. Tranga's tits still looked like the eyes on a drunken Mister Potato Head. Lord, she was an angry woman…

Then there was Quan, again… He had been lanced by a scorpion on the head of his…well, let's just say a place no man wants to be seriously stung by anything. His entire undercarriage had swollen up like a mango fruit basket. He could barely walk without groaning. The only good news was, for some reason, he hadn't died from what was supposed to be a deadly black scorpion sting.

And Will and I knew absolutely nothing about these two. But we would…

CHAPTER NINETEEN

At this point, our wayward bounty hunters decided that discretion was the better part of valor and they retreated from the emergency room to their hostel. But their anger over the fiasco they'd been through…again…was burning them alive. They'd never had anything remotely like this happen to them. But they both admitted that this whole thing was growing old. After all, they were being beaten to pieces and they'd never even been close to their targets. They had reached a point where they wanted a confrontation. Face to face. *Mano a mano.* They wanted to see the eyes of those people when they hurt them. They decided that tomorrow they would take Will and me out, personally, once and for all. If they felt well enough…

The following day, Quan and Tranga were both feeling better but not good. It was obvious that they were going to need another day for a little more recuperation before they waged a final war on the two stinkin' *Americanos.*

It was just as well. We were gone. We had things to do in Miami.

■ ■ ■

Early the following morning, Travis and Cody picked up a personnel transport vehicle from Homestead Air Reserve Base, and a handful of Army uniforms. They met with Will, Diego, Jing, and me (and a fairly nervous Key West tattooist), all in my rental car, at a prearranged gas station. My friends changed into the uniforms Travis had procured. They all looked very official. The tattooist hid in the back of the military truck. Travis drove the truck and I drove my car.

It was midday when we arrived at the office building housing the chemical analysis company. I had our three bottles of Crazy Grow juice. At that point, we parked the vehicles in the planned location in the underground parking lot, then Travis, Cody, and I headed up to the company offices with the three bottles. The rest of the team stayed in the truck in the parking lot.

The mafioso leader, Batino Tenseno, was standing by the large window of the lab, staring out, his dark eyes scanning the grounds. His long dark hair was pulled back into a ponytail. There was no more conscience in those eyes than the last time our team had seen him. "Lizard eyes..." Jing had called them. There was, however, a gash across his cheekbone that had only just begun to heal. (Compliments of Travis Christian, from the last time they had met in an elevator here.) Once again, there were the two big guys within quick reach of him. The same ones as before — crew cuts, large shoulders, cold eyes — but they too were sporting a number of cuts and bruises that hadn't managed to heal yet — also compliments of our soldier friend during their last "visit" in the elevator.

But most importantly, standing between them was Tax, my son, apparently no worse for the wear. He looked at me and our eyes locked, saying wonderful things that weren't spoken often enough.

Off to the side stood the very nervous technician with whom we'd been working all this time.

There was a good deal of tension in the air when Travis walked in, followed by Cody and me. The heavies were reaching for their guns. Their boss waved them down but their stares could have melted ice. Everyone knew this wasn't over. (The mafia people had obviously hoped Travis might not come back from the mission in Panama.)

The little chemist guy broke the tension. Looking at the bag Travis carried, he said as casually as possible, "So, you found more of the formula, huh?"

My friend nodded, addressing him and the mafia people. "Yeah, three more bottles, but I think it's pretty safe to say that's all you're going to find on this planet."

"So, we'll take them. Now," said the mafioso boss, who nodded at his people and they reluctantly released Tax.

When Tax reached me, we hugged shamelessly. The world was round again. Travis sat down the small, padded travel case with the last three bottles of the Crazy Grow, and slid it across the linoleum floor with his foot.

The boss man opened it and looked inside, then closed it and looked up at the chemist. "Test it." He pulled a pistol from a shoulder holster then. "Nobody leaves until I know."

"It's a simple test," said the chemist, trying to keep all the balls in the air here, and trying to keep from getting killed in the process. "Give me five minutes."

Everyone gave him the five uncomfortable minutes. He came back, sweat stains under his armpits, but exceedingly pleased. He looked at the mafioso. "It's the real thing. It's good, just like the others. All three bottles." The little guy exhaled and held out his hands. "The final tests for replication still aren't in, but we're hoping for a nucleic pathway to reproduce this. But nothing is for sure at this point. We've got to hope for the best. This could be one of the most important discoveries of this century."

"Okay, okay," growled the headman. "You get it worked out with what you're given. You keep the half-bottle for tests. We'll take the first bottle you had and the three new ones."

"But…" stuttered the chemist. "What if the temperature…"

The mafioso's eyes went hard. "We'll keep it cozy and cool. Get it. Now!" He held up a finger. "And don't even dream about scamming me here. And you better not need more. *Capiche?"*

Once the technician returned, and all four bottles were secured, the mafioso offered a final glare at us, then his people picked up the bag and they backed their way out of the room.

Gone but not forgotten. It was showtime…

As soon as the three Miami mobsters were out the office doors, Travis brought up his phone. "The game is on," he growled. "They're on their way out and entering the elevator. We want the case they're carrying — and be careful with that, understand?"

■ ■ ■

When the mafia boss and his people reached the covered ground floor and cautiously exited the elevator, they noticed there was a small U.S. Army transport vehicle — the type often used to move prisoners or important personnel — sitting fairly close to their vehicle. The hood on the motor was popped and a soldier appeared to be working on it. They couldn't see the other two crouched inside the rear of the vehicle.

The mafia boss and his two men took a cautious glance at the soldier and kept moving. Authorities of any sort made them nervous. They passed the truck and were walking toward their car when one of the back doors of the military vehicle opened quietly and two "soldiers" reared up and fired their small CO_2 pistols — no noise, just the *pffftt* that a compressed air weapon makes — then pulled the door closed. It all took no more than five seconds. At the same time, the third soldier (with her long blond hair tucked under her cap), turned from the engine and popped the mafioso himself in the back, then set the gun back on the engine block and returned to what she was doing. The big man and his people jerked from the sting of the darts (which had been soaked overnight in curare*)* and glanced around. But there was no gunman, no enemy, just the slim fellow working at the engine. They all, almost simultaneously, reached back around to the distinct pain in their backs. It took a few moments, but they finally managed to pull out the darts.

The three men looked at each other and blinked a couple of times, on guard now, but the curare was already sliding into their veins. They glanced over at the truck, where the soldier was still busy inside the engine cowling.

"This is not right," muttered Batino Tenseno, blinking again. "I'm not liking this. We need to get to the car." But he was already slurring his words slightly, and his soldiers, although nodding in agreement, were wavering now. They stood there for a moment but it seemed like they were stuck in mud. Finally, one of the soldiers turned and took a couple of steps, but that was as far as he got. It was like he just ran out of gas. All three of them were standing still, tilting like drunks, eyes getting distant, their breathing getting slower. The case with the bottles slipped from the head man's fingers and slid gently to the floor. In just moments, the two guards dropped to their knees, hands falling to their sides, eyes seriously confused but laced with growing concern. Then they just collapsed onto their faces, their hands not even coming up in protection.

The mafioso boss was the last to go. He too was on his knees now. He paused and looked at Jing, who had turned from the engine and was staring at him. A final moment of realization drifted across his eyes. She smiled evilly and wiggled her fingers in goodbye just before the man dropped face-first onto the pavement.

Just about that time the elevator doors on the underground parking area opened again, and Travis, Cody, and I — and most importantly, Tax — walked out.

Things had gone well. Remarkably well. But as for the mafia boss and his two junkyard dogs, not so good. And for them, this was just the beginning of a story with a really bad ending.

Cody grabbed the case with the bottles as a couple of us dragged the three mafia men over to the transport and threw them in with the tattoo artist. Travis pulled a piece of paper from his breast pocket and handed it to the man.

"You've got your portable equipment. This is what I want on their chests. It doesn't have to be fancy, but I want it...*loud.* You've got an hour before we're back at Homestead Air Force Base."

Long story short, the trip to Homestead was uneventful. Curare has a way of doing that to you. There was a big C-124 Globemaster military transport plane preparing for departure to Iraq within the hour — one of the many flying in and out right now, given the hoopla in the Middle East. Reservations had been secured by Travis' colonel friend. The three freshly tattooed fellows were bound securely and loaded aboard.

The salient point to remember here was that this was 1991, and America and its allies had just decided that enough was enough with a fellow by the name of Saddam Hussein in the Middle East. Half of the sensible world was in the process of kicking Iraq's ass in what came to be known as the Persian Gulf War and Operation Desert Storm.

The *Reader's Digest* version of this event took the mafia people on a long plane ride, ending at a hot, bumpy, bulldozed airstrip in the middle of the Iraqi desert. The Americans had done what they needed to do — pretty much crushed the backbone of Saddam's army. At this particular military fuel and ammo location, they had taken down their tents, loaded their equipment, and pulled out. Saddam's remaining forces were headed this way in an unorganized, but vindictive rout.

Later that same day, as their recent transportation flew off into the sunset, Batino Tenseno and his companions gradually came around from their heavy, curare-induced comas, and found themselves in nothing but their underwear in the middle of a desert in the middle of Iraq, in the closing pages of Operation Desert Storm. That was bad enough, but about then, they were spotted by a group of Saddam Hussein's retreating military — very unhappy folks and bitterly disposed toward Americans.

At that particular point, there were probably few things worse, to tell you the truth, than being a weaponless, damned near stark naked American in the middle of the desert with an American forces helmet strapped on your head and *Screw Saddam Hussein And The Camel He Rode In On!* tattooed boldly across your chest… Timing is everything.

CHAPTER TWENTY

All that ends well, ends well, someone once said. I think… And indeed, the whole magic juice/Panamanian island prison/mafia fiasco seemed to have ended fairly well. We had placed the last four bottles of our magnificent formula in my environmentally controlled bank safety deposit box (and left a few ounces with the chemist in Miami). They were secure for the moment, until we decided what to do with them.

That afternoon, while I was in Key West, I helped Diego rent an apartment. He was going to be here for a while, and he needed a place of his own. I found him a nice used car as well. He deserved it. We lucked out and the whole thing took little more than a couple of hours.

I was personally looking forward to a couple of days of beer and sunsets, and a girl or two if possible. Will agreed, and early that evening he came up to my place on Big Pine to start with the "beer and sunset" part. Later, we thought we'd try Marathon for a little fun and games. Little did we know that the evening's entertainment had already arrived on Big Pine and was headed our way.

■ ■ ■

It was just about dark. The sun had surrendered in the west and the first silver vestiges of an early March moon were rising in the east. We figured one more beer and we'd hop into Will's little Mustang and head for the girls of Marathon. I'd spent part of the day with Shadow, catching up with my boy, but he was gone right now, probably out on one of his jaunts with Cielo.

But...during the day, while we were in Miami solving magic juice problems, the Last Resort's two hit people had found themselves in a world of disappointment. Their pride had been shattered (by nothing more than circumstance, really), and all they had in its place was a hell of a lot of sore and no money. What they wanted now was a shot of revenge.

Quan and Tranga had driven up to Big Pine Key and popped a few tequilas at the Big Pine Inn, followed by a couple of the doctor's pain pills, just to get their confidence in place. In the process, they had double-checked the phone book and found where I lived. I was first on their list. It was to be a night of vindication, which would hopefully whitewash several instances of miserable timing, bad luck, and considerable pain. Tranga had procured a pistol from a pawn shop earlier in the day, and they now intended a more direct solution.

Will and I were sitting in lounge chairs on the deck, staring at the moon, and I was occasionally flipping my coin from Rufus (which consistently seemed to come up tails...strangest damned thing I'd ever seen) when we heard something behind us, from the stairs. It sounded like an evil chuckle.

And actually, it was...

We both swung around and there before us were two people. Asian folks, it appeared, but odd in the respect that they both had the exact same face. But man, I swear, as they moved up, they looked like something between really bad luck and a train wreck. The guy was dragging one leg like something out of a Mel Brooks Frankenstein movie, and he had a significant twitch in his left eye. The woman was clearly damaged as well. She had a good selection of bruises and bandages, and her fairly large breasts seemed to seriously dislike each other. She looked like a poster child for Drunken Cosmetic Surgeons Anonymous.

I glanced at Will. He shrugged and shook his head. "I got no idea," he whispered.

"Aaahhh, we got you now! You gonna pay now, mons!" cried the guy as he started to pull a gun from his pants. Then he screamed (when the barrel sight caught on his scorpion-poisoned dick).

Will and I flinched at the scream.

"Whoa, cowboy, whoa," muttered Will, bringing up his hands, palms out. "I'd like someone to explain this to me, 'cause right now, I'm real uncomfortable. What did we do to offend you, dude?"

"You sure you got the right place?" I said, straightening up slowly in my chair.

"Oh, we got da right place! Oh, yah, mon! Yah mon!" growled Quan, lips quivering, a little spittle forming at the edges of his mouth and splashing outward. "We got da right place!"

Will and I eased back a bit in case the guy was rabid. I accidentally huffed out a slight exclamation.

The guy brought up his gun. "So, you think dis be funny, huh? Huh, mon? Funny? Dis be nothing." He leaned in and shook the gun at us. "I got a dick da size of a football — and not in a good way. I got nuts da size of grapefruit!"

I shrugged, trying to defuse this. "Well, in some circles that might be impressive. Have you considered porn movies?"

That didn't help. He shot a hole in the deck in front of me.

"You don't know me, mista. But you got big trouble comin', mon, and den we gonna collect from Madam Sharee after all!"

Sharee! Sharee Chaleen! Our Jamaican Last Resort nemesis.

I looked at Will and there was no question that he got the message as well. The damned woman was paying to have us hit!

"So…maybe you be havin' some sort of magic jumba that preserve you," the fellow hissed. "But not now, mon. Not no more!" The crazed guy was bringing up the gun again, almost as if he forgot he had it. He fired another round between us into the deck. "I spit on your magic jumba! I spit on it!"

The fellow was shaking the pistol at us again, his glazed eyes seriously wild now. I could see Will preparing to launch himself from the chair. What the hell, we had nothing left to lose…

But at that moment, a shadowy wraith came soaring out of the darkness — a fairly large wraith with nearly a five-foot wingspan and serious talons. It just clipped him on the head. The pass seemed almost effortless. But it doesn't take much for an osprey talon to wreck your day.

Quan screamed. The gun went off again, leaving Will and me diving for cover. But the shot was more of a reflex than anything else. Cielo's claw had caught just the edge of Quan's scalp. But the pain and the image were more than enough, especially when it was backed by Shadow, my 150-pound shepherd-Rottweiler mix, who was bounding up the stairs like pain on wheels, roaring like a lion.

The cavalry had arrived just in time…

Both of our assailants took one look at this situation, then screamed in remarkably good harmony, scrambled backward, and simply hurled themselves over the porch rail and off the deck like crazed *Titanic* rats. It was nearly ten feet to the ground, but adrenaline and fear are an amazing combination. By the time we had our two rescuers at bay, the Jamaican hitsters were in their car and screeching away. Tranga had a badly sprained ankle, and Quan had a small section of his scalp that was going to have to be tacked down at the emergency room (where they were getting to be regulars).

In the end, this proved to be enough for this resilient Jamaican duo. There was just no percentage in swimming against a tide of incredibly bad luck here. They were going to head home. Back to the land of perfect sunsets, swaying palms, and easily duped tourists.

Ya, mon…Miss Chaleen could chase these sonabitches herself!

The following morning, they took stock of the situation and decided they were running out of places to hurt. They called Miss Chaleen and told her she could keep her money, then packed up and caught the first plane home.

There are times when discretion is simply the better part of valor.

■ ■ ■

The following day, as the sun set in the west (as it does in all good cowboy movies), the Hole in the Coral Wall Gang gathered around our table at Crazy Eddie's. It had been a remarkable adventure, again. Hell, several remarkable adventures, actually.

We raised our drinks and cheered ourselves, then poured a splash of each of our drinks on the table for the gods, who once again had watched over us.

(*While we all suspected there was just one big guy watching, we took pleasure in the old ritual of sailors and pirates.)*

But, as pleasurable as the evening was, with great recollections of luck and valor in this last adventure, it still rolled around to the big question: What do we do with our four bottles of magic juice…a concoction that had the potential to preserve the world?

It just so happened that I had received a call from the chemist at Organic Analysis Incorporated in Miami that morning. It was a disappointing conversation, at least to this point. The chemist fellow we'd been dealing with was nervous to stuttering because he figured between us and the mafia people, he was in a serious "rock and a hard place" situation, and he didn't have good news.

None of us really thought he was spoofing us. I was sure he had seen the surveillance videos of the mafia guys being taken out in the downstairs garage (and because there was no sound, he and his people assumed they had been killed). So he was "peeing in his pants" cooperative. It's just that it wasn't the best of news. It was like the girl of your dreams telling you she wanted to marry you…but just not right now.

He explained to me, "We've given it our best efforts, and we have one of the top labs in the country, and again, some of the elements in this formula we recognize and can reproduce, but damn…this is still like apples and oranges and golf balls…" He paused. "We can blend apples and oranges but we still can't blend them with golf balls." He sighed. "The chemical formula for this stuff is literally out of this world. While we understand some of it, we would still struggle to reproduce it, at least at this point." He paused once more. "We would like to continue our work on this, if you would let us. I can promise you that we will continue in ultra-secrecy."

I decided to press him, just to make sure he got the message. "You've met my friends…you understand that if there's any indiscretion here…death would be like a gift. A favor…"

I swear I heard the guy hiss out a gasp from where I was, but sometimes the fear of God is a good thing.

So, the bottom line: The good news was, we had four bottles of the most amazing planet-changing juice in our known world. The bad news was, we probably weren't going to get more in the near future. So, there was absolutely no point in trying to develop or market a product you possessed a very limited quantity of.

But the other good news was, given the fact that it only took a couple of drops in a gallon of water for it to work in a normal but remarkable fashion, four bottles would go a long way in a critical situation on this planet. It might indeed be a civilization saver or starter in the right circumstances.

The big question was, who should be in control of something this vitally important? None of us felt comfortable giving this to the government — not with its track record of selling, losing, or disappearing things.

It was Cody who came up with a fairly viable solution. Oddly enough, he had a friend who worked for a special agency — a post-apocalyptic organization that served as somewhat of a backup for humanity. The Future Farmers Alliance was affiliated closely with a few groups around the world that collected and stored large numbers of seeds of valuable, life-preserving vegetables and fruits. In particular, they partnered with a major genetic resource preservation organization in Colorado, which was home to one of the world's largest plant and animal gene banks.

Cody explained that his friend's organization also partnered with a Rocky Mountain seed alliance group — a nonprofit team working to create a network of seed growers, distributors, and educators in the western Rocky Mountain region of the United States.

Cody Joe was on a roll and no one got in his way. He explained that his friend's people were also affiliated with one of the international centers for tropical agriculture in Colombia, which focused on promoting agrobiodiversity and sustainable agroecosystems in Africa, Asia, Latin America, and the Caribbean. In a bad situation, the ability to preserve the world would lie in the hands of people like these.

Cody paused and looked around at us. "I know all this may seem strange, coming from a guy like me. But somebody has to consider the possibilities. Somebody has to think about the future, and that's what these people are doing. These are the folks whose hindsight and foresight could very well preserve the planet." He eased out a sigh and smiled. "Who knows? Maybe one of these days I may want to get married and have children. If that happens, I want there to be a future for them." He grinned again. "I want to be able to tell them to eat their vegetables or I'll beat their asses!"

I shook my head. "What a gift something like this concoction would be to organizations like these you've mentioned. What a jump start it would be to mankind if something really went south on parts of this planet for a while."

"Besides," Will muttered. "How much more money do any of us need? We're all wealthier than King Tut now, anything past that is just pure, ugly greed."

"No Crazy Grow company then, I guess…" growled Eddie, obviously a little disappointed.

"Nope, probably no Crazy Grow," we all replied.

"Can this friend of yours be trusted, do you think?" Travis asked Cody, bringing us back to earth, as always. "With something of this magnitude?"

"Can anyone really be trusted *always* with everything?" replied his buddy. "Sometimes you just have to close your eyes, think nice thoughts, and roll the dice…"

"I'll talk to him when we get that far along," rumbled Travis. "I'll help him see Jesus in all this."

■ ■ ■

While Cody spent some time visiting with his friend at Future Farmers Alliance, the rest of us were ready to kick back for a little while. But unfortunately, Will and I had one last issue to resolve — Miss Chaleen and the Last Resort, who seemed to go by the Canadian Mounties' slogan, "They always get their man." (Or woman.)

We had a couple of possibilities here: We could continue to be on guard for whoever they sent next to collect money or we could go back to the Last Resort and try to resolve this, work out an acceptable percentage (which I felt was blackmail), or maybe help Chaleen develop a conscience — one way or another.

We had paid five thousand dollars each (which was a hell of a lot of money to begin with), and apparently, according to Will (who felt he now had it figured out), we were supposed to have paid Chaleen five thousand more each when we rode off peacefully into the sunset to meet God, hopefully… Which hadn't happened. But in Chaleen's words, a contract was a contract. It didn't matter if we didn't understand it. It didn't matter if we didn't die on time. And certainly, several tries at that part had been arranged.

We were over at Will's houseboat, sitting on the deck, drinking beer and trading ideas regarding this dilemma, when Will offered a possible solution.

"What if you could talk her into a coin toss?" he said with a smile.

I had been rolling my coin from Rufus between my fingers as I gazed out at the blue-green gulf in the distance, offering an occasional flip. I studied the coin for a minute, then looked up at him. "The coin never misses. It's always tails on a legitimate toss. But how do we get her to take heads?"

"We can't," my friend said with a trollish grin. "If she picks tails and it lands like that, we shoot her."

I couldn't tell whether he was joking or not, but the bottom line was, Chaleen obviously had no qualms about taking us out for not meeting her image of the contract. We needed to resolve this before she succeeded.

CHAPTER TWENTY-ONE

The following day we were packing our gear for a quick trip back to that little paradoxical island off the corner of Jamaica. *Back to the velvet lion's den.* We gave a heads-up to the team, letting them know where we were going and the name of the…*lady*…who ran it, and that we weren't planning on being gone any longer than a couple of days. We also told the team we would check in every twelve hours. If they didn't hear from us religiously, on the button, there was a problem.

We took my Cessna 182 floatplane, and the trip went smoothly. We refueled in Kingston, then skipped across to the island of last resorts and dropped into their little runway. By the time the prop had quit clicking there was a jeep waiting for us, the same big Jamaican at the wheel as before. He cocked his head as we came over, staring at us incredulously.

"You boys come back for another shot at being dead, huh?" He shook his mane of dreadlocks. "I don' know why you be here, mons, but you must have coconuts for *cojones*…or shit for brains…" He offered what was almost a grin. "We hear about da hunters Miss Chaleen send for you. Dey be seriously unhappy souls. But you gonna need some serious juju or a pocketful of cash, I hear, to survive da day."

Once again, the jeep dropped us off at the front of the complex. We looked at each other, shrugged, and headed for Miss Chaleen's office. I knocked, Will grabbed the handle, and we entered. We were over being nice but there was one last role to play here.

Sharee Chaleen was sitting at her large desk, shuffling some papers, pretending she hadn't known we were there from the moment the wheels on the plane touched down. She looked up and offered a raised eyebrow. "Well, I'm surprised to see you two."

"Surprised to see us, or surprised to see us *alive?"* countered Will.

She ignored the comeback. "Well, have you two finally decided to stop by and pay your outstanding bills?"

"Let's just say we've come to talk with you about them," I said. "Maybe offer you a solution." I paused. "There's a big gulf between what you think we should pay and why we should pay at all. But like I said, there might be a solution. Depends on if you're a woman of spirit — willing to play to chance a little." My face became serious. "You're smart enough to know that we have serious friends, and if you've done your homework, you know that revenge is one of their favorite sports."

"So...you've come to threaten me rather than pay me?" Sharee replied. "Not a good idea when you're on my island..."

"We've given it some thought," I said. "We're gamblers by nature, and so are you. So, we have a simple solution." I paused and stared at her. "Why not a gamble? How about a simple coin toss? The ten thousand dollars you claim we owe you against us walking away with our heads on our shoulders and you call off your dogs...forever. On one toss of a coin... Because the truth is, this tit-for-tat here is gonna get really messy at some point pretty soon."

It was a gamble regardless. We had to coax the woman in the right direction. I pressed my luck and drew out my special "always tails" coin from Rufus. I flipped it into the air and caught it, then tossed her the coin with the image of an ugly snake for tails and a beautiful woman's face on the heads side. There was no question that heads was psychologically beguiling to begin with... It landed on her desktop.

"Heads the woman, tails the snake," I said casually. "Or your choice, of course." *I thought I was being clever...because most people by far instinctively chose the attractive woman. The image of the snake just didn't promote confidence.*

Miss Chaleen picked up the coin and studied it for a few moments — longer than I liked. She flipped it into the air, caught it deftly, then studied it again. Then she looked at us and smiled. "Very well, sirs," she said. "I'll accept your challenge. But I'll take the snake and tails, and it drops to the floor."

Will hissed out a breath as Chaleen continued.

"Actually, I've always had an interest in coinage, especially ancient coins. Especially those that go back as far as the Mesopotamians and Sumerians — peoples who dealt with forces and powers that we have little understanding of today." She drew a breath. "Some say they were able to invest abilities into inert objects, like jewelry and coinage. Unique abilities..."

I heard my partner issue something not repeatable under his breath. He glanced at me, his eyes carrying "gallows" disappointment. We were screwed. I was willing to bet now that this woman knew way more than we did about coins and this situation. And I remembered Rufus's words... *"Maybe once in a thousand tosses..."*

It really wasn't the money — ten thousand dollars wasn't going to break us in any fashion. It was losing the damned bet. It was the failure at the cleverness and guile that we enjoyed so much. *For God's sake, the damned woman had been willing to kill us for a few freaking dollars! And now she was going to take our money...*

But a bet was a bet, and according to Miss Chaleen, a contract was a contract.

She straightened up and smiled again. "I'll take tails."

Yep, we were totally screwed...

Ultimately, there was no putting off the inevitable — it was lambs to the slaughter. Miss Chaleen offered another of her superior smiles, then stepped around her desk into the middle of the room, and without much more ado than a superior smile, she took a breath, exhaled, and tossed the coin into the air. The look of confidence on the face of our nemesis was purely deflating.

The coin went up and the coin came down, clattering on the Spanish tile floor, pirouetting for a moment, then collapsing into a spinning clangor, then gradually slowing to a point that allowed us to determine what the gods had decided. It finally stopped and we all gasped.

It was heads! The stately ancient woman stared up at us from the floor. It was heads!

"Son of a bitch," whispered Will incredulously. "Son of a bitch! That's amazing."

We all just stood there for a moment — Chaleen soaked in shock and us bathed in impossible delight.

I could almost hear Rufus chuckling somewhere, and I was reminded of what he had last said to me, "*Maybe once in every thousand tosses, mon, it might go heads... Maybe... But never rule anything out because impossibility and coincidence are da gods' favorite wines...*"

Chaleen, our curator of entertainment and death, had gone pale, her breathing shallow, her eyes wide and simply disbelieving. *These were just not odds that someone beat. She knew of the coin. She knew its history. There had to be a mistake here. Somehow, she'd been played...*

She bent down slowly, picked up the coin, and examined it again incredulously.

I let her have a moment, then I gently reached over and took my coin from her. I couldn't dredge up any pity for a woman who had tried to kill me without my consent...several times.

"You win some, you lose some," I said. "Death may be the last resort for some, but it's way down on my list of things to do yet. I hope you remember that, because a deal's a deal..."

The woman stepped back and leaned against her desk, deflated, eyes distant and a touch off-center, seriously disappointed she wasn't going to get to kill someone or take their money (which had become her two favorite things in life).

Besides, she was certain our friends knew where we were and what we were doing, and truthfully, there were a couple of people in that group she just couldn't risk taking on.

We left Miss Sharee Chaleen, strange curator of death and peace for some (as long as the bill was paid in full and all the i's were dotted in the contract), still leaning against her desk, bathed in a good degree of bitter disappointment. There was a sense of, if not defeat, at least discouragement in the woman that left me feeling fairly confident we'd seen the last of her.

Half an hour later, we were lifting off, leaving the beautiful beaches, crystal waters, tennis courts, golf courses, bars, and ballrooms of the Last Resort.

It was all a rather clever idea, I suppose — death delivered inconspicuously, maybe nearly painless and pleasantly. But there was a part of me that said when the time came, I wanted to meet death on my own terms. I wanted to stare it in the face, scrap a little, and maybe at the end, offer the devil a coin toss for my soul.

When Will and I finally returned, the whole team gathered together at Eddie's for one final post-mission meeting. We had journeyed across the southern hemisphere a couple of times, waged war, been battered by lies, and saved by truths. We'd discovered the impossible, lost it, then found it again, then had given it away. But once again through it all, we had rediscovered the faith, the affection, and the undeniable bonds we carried for each other. We were, if nothing else, through all the fire and brimstone, the truths and the lies, a most remarkable group. We were…*the Hole in the Coral Wall Gang.*

I hope you have enjoyed this novel. If you would like to be added to my mailing list (to stay apprised of new novels and to receive bimonthly updates and my newspaper columns), email me at: reisig@ipa.net

—Michael Reisig

And…be sure to read the rest of
Michael Reisig's best-selling

ROAD TO KEY WEST SERIES

THE ROAD TO KEY WEST

The Road to Key West is an adventurous, humorous sojourn that cavorts its way through the 1970s Caribbean, from Key West and the Bahamas to Cuba and Central America—a Caribbean brew of part-time pirates, heartless larcenists, wild women, Voodoo bokors, drug smugglers, and a wacky Jamaican soothsayer.

Kindle Book only $3.99
To Preview or Purchase this book on amazon.com, use this link:
http://www.amazon.com/dp/B004RPMYF8

BACK ON THE ROAD TO KEY WEST
The Golden Scepter — Book II

An ancient map and a lost pirate treasure, a larcenous Bahamian scoundrel with his gang of cutthroats, a wild and crazy journey into South America in search of a magical antediluvian device, and perilous, hilarious encounters with outlandish villains and zany friends will keep you locked to your seat and giggling maniacally.

ALONG THE ROAD TO KEY WEST
The Truthmaker — Book III

Fast-paced humor and adventure with wacky pilots, quirky con men, mad villains, bold women, and a gadget to die for. Florida Keys adventurers Kansas Stamps and Will Bell find their lives turned upside down when they discover a truth device hidden in the temple of an ancient civilization. Enthralled by the virtue of personally dispensing truth and justice with this unique tool, they soon discover everyone wants what they have—from the government to the Vatican.

SOMEWHERE ON THE ROAD TO KEY WEST
The Emerald Cave — Book IV

The captivating diary of an amateur archaeologist sends our intrepid explorers on a journey into the heart of the Panamanian jungle in search of *la cueva de Esmeralda* (the Emerald Cave), and a lost Spanish treasure. But local brigand Tu Phat Shong and his gang of cutthroats are searching for the same treasure. If that wasn't enough, one of the Caribbean's nastiest drug lords has a score to settle with our reluctant heroes.

Kindle Book only $3.99
To Preview or Purchase this book on amazon.com, use this link:
http://www.amazon.com/dp/B00NOABMKA

DOWN THE ROAD TO KEY WEST
Pancho Villa's Gold — Book V

If you're looking for clever fun with zany characters, a and electric high adventure, this one's for you! Reisig's newest offering is guaranteed to keep you locked to your seat and slapping at the pages, while burbling up a giggle or two. In the fifth book of this series, our reluctant Caribbean heroes find themselves competing for the affections of a beautiful antiquities dealer and searching for the lost treasure of Mexico's most renowned desperado.

Kindle Book only $3.99
To Preview or Purchase this book on amazon.com, use this link:
http://www.amazon.com/dp/B01EPI6XY4

BEYOND THE ROAD TO KEY WEST
Mayan Gold — Book VI

First, the reader is drawn back over 400 years, to the magnificent Mayan empire — to the intrigue of powerful rulers, Spanish invasion, and an adventure/love story that survives the challenge of time. Moving forward several centuries, Kansas and Will stumble upon a collection of ancient writings, and the tale of a treasure that was cached by the great Mayan ruler, Nachán Can…

Kindle book only 3.99
To Preview or Purchase this book on amazon.com, use this link:
http://www.amazon.com/dp/B01M293NDP

A FAR ROAD TO KEY WEST
Emeralds and Lies — Book VII

The "Hole in the Coral Wall Gang" return to the Guatemalan jungle to retrieve the remainder of a Mayan king's incredible treasure, but in the process they find themselves engaged in a grassroots revolution, pursued by a vengeful colonel in the Guatemalan military, and immersed in the intrigue of a World War Two Nazi treasure. Then, there's the beautiful sister of a revolutionary, the golden Swiss francs, and the greatest challenge of all — *Granja Penal de Pavón* — the most terrifying prison in all of Central America.

To Preview or Purchase this book on amazon.com, use this link:
http://www.amazon.com/dp/B072VRR2VY

THE WILD ROAD TO KEY WEST
The Cave of The Stars — Book VIII

Once again, the Hole in the Coral Wall Gang is wrapped in a wild adventure. Diamonds and emeralds, a lost city infused by a treasure and an ancient race, a secret cave with a timeless message, ruthless bandits, jungle Indians, and nefarious cowboys are all part of this non-stop roller coaster ride.

Did I mention the gang's new guide, Arturio — a Venezuelan outback opportunist who has a mild obsession with Russian Roulette? Or Passi, the lustful jungle witch who just can't make up her mind?

To Preview or Purchase this book on amazon.com, use this link::
www.amazon.com/dp/B078FMD5TZ

A PIRATE'S ROAD TO KEY WEST
Lafitte's Gold Book — Book IX

In the ninth novel of his best-selling "Road To Key West" series, Michael Reisig once again locks his readers into a careening odyssey of hidden fortunes, mercurial romance, conscienceless villains, and bizarre friends.

From Caracas to New Orleans, into the dark fringes of Haiti, down through the Windward Islands, then back into the Florida Keys, Kansas Stamps, Will Bell, and the Hole in the Coral Wall Gang chase a stolen pre-Columbian treasure. Then there's the Voodoo-practicing drug boss, a vengeful Colombian don, and a highly artful assassin. Before you can catch your breath, it all rolls together into a turbulent Key West Fantasy Fest finale.

To Preview or Purchase this book on amazon.com, use this link:
https://www.amazon.com/PIRATES-ROAD-KEY-WEST/dp/0999091476

THE LOST ROAD TO KEY WEST
The Pharaoh's Gold — Book X

Take a wild journey, from ancient Egyptian explorations to modern-day discoveries in the walls of the mystical Grand Canyon. It's history and mythology mixed with hard-hitting real time adventure. Did I mention, the osprey, and the "hit girls" and the gold?

To Preview or Purchase this book on amazon.com, use this link: https://amzn.to/2z2oo8w

THE INCREDIBLE KEY WEST-CARIBBEAN RACE

Kansas stamps and Will Bell are back in an absolutely roaring Caribbean adventure that may be the most unique of Reisig's tales to date.

After a night of Key West carousing, the boys find themselves entangled in a contest of sorts — a race, or perhaps more correctly, a series of challenges that carry them across the Caribbean and into Central and South America. (We're talking about villainous villains, wild Texan promoters, hit men, biker gangs, beautiful crazy women, mad Colombian dons, moonlit voodoo ceremonies, sailing races and hurricanes, and an island with creatures that would keep your nightmares awake.)

Kindle Book only $2.99
To Preview or Purchase this book on amazon.com, use this link: https://www.amazon.com/Incredible-Key-West-Caribbean-Race/dp/057870207X

GODS GUNS AND MONEY ON THE ROAD TO KEY WEST

White-knuckle airplane crashes; wild, lustful Amazonians; bungled bank thefts; river pirates; remarkable dogs and hawks; an ancient crystal skull; diamond thieves, drug lords, and an amazing "Animal Man."

In what may well be Michael Reisig's most entertaining effort yet comes a wild adventure that carries the reader from South Florida into the Caribbean, down to South America, and back again. Intertwined through the read are the questions we ask ourselves when we look up at the stars, as well as a theme of the sometimes extraordinary connections we experience with the lesser creatures that share this planet with us. Everything in between is just heart-hammering, page-ripping action.

Kindle Book only $2.99
To Preview or Purchase this book on amazon.com, use this link:
https://www.amazon.com/Gods-Guns-Money-Road-West/dp/1736347918

THE TRUE TALES OF THE ROAD TO KEY WEST

These tales will make you smile with wonder, remind you of the importance of loyalty and love in life, and make you laugh your ass off. I have taken my experiences, encounters, and adventures, and blended them into and around the highlights of my eight "Road To Key West" novels. Included in the package are a number of memory-jarring photos and terrific quotes, to create a humorous, insightful, walk down memory lane for new and seasoned readers.

If you haven't read any of "The Road To Key West" novels, this is the perfect place to begin. If you've read them all, you'll love these engaging, sometimes laugh-out-loud recollections.

Also, be sure to read...

CARIBBEAN GOLD
THE TREASURE OF TORTUGA

In 1668, Englishman Trevor Holte and the audacious freebooter Clevin Greymore sail from the Port of London for the West Indies. They set out in search of adventure and wealth, but the challenges they encounter are beyond their wildest dreams—the brutal Spanish, ruthless buccaneers, a pirate king, the lure of Havana, and the women, as fierce in their desires as Caribbean storms. And then, there was the gold—wealth beyond imagination. But some treasures outlive the men who bury them…

Kindle Book only $3.99
To Preview or Purchase this book on amazon.com, use this link:
http://www.amazon.com/dp/B00S8SR0WW

CARIBBEAN GOLD
THE TREASURE OF TIME

In the spring of 1980, three adventurers set out from Key West in search of a lost treasure on the Isle of Tortuga, off the coast of Haiti. Equipped with an ancient parchment and a handful of clues, they embark on a journey that carries them back across time, challenging their courage and their imaginations, presenting them with remarkable allies and pitting them against an amalgam of unrelenting enemies. In the process, they uncover far more than a treasure. They discover the power of friendship and faith, the unflagging capacity of spirit, and come to realize that some things are forever…

Kindle Book only $3.99
To Preview or Purchase this book on amazon.com, use this link:
http://www.amazon.com/dp/B00S8SR0WW

CARIBBEAN GOLD
THE TREASURE OF MARGARITA

The Treasure of Margarita spans three centuries of high adventure. Beginning in 1692, in the pirate stronghold of Port Royal, it carries the reader across the Southern Hemisphere in a collage of rip-roaring escapades. Then it soars forward five generations, into modern-day intrigue and romance in Key West and the Caribbean.

A staggering fortune of Spanish black pearls and a 300-year-old letter with a handful of clues set the course that Travis Christian and William Cody embark upon. But it's not an easy sail. Seasoned with remarkable women and bizarre villains, the adventure ricochets from one precarious situation to the next.

Made in the USA
Monee, IL
16 May 2022